LAST CALL FOR A DEADLY DIVA

FLO ANTHONY

WAHIDA CLARK
PRESENTS
INNOVATIVE PUBLISHING

Wahida Clark Presents Publishing 60 Evergreen Place
Suite 904
East Orange, New Jersey 07018
1(866)910-6920
www.WClarkPublishing.com

Library of Congress Cataloging-In-Publication Data: Last Call For a Deadly Diva/ by Flo Anthony

ISBN (paperback): 978-1-954161-66-5

ISBN (eBook): 978-1-954161-67-2

ISBN (audio): 978-1-954161-68-9

ACKNOWLEDGMENTS

First, I want to thank God and my late parents, Joe and Doris Johnson Anthony, for giving me life and always encouraging my creativity.

Thank you, Wahida Clark, for your belief in me and support. You are the best publisher and the baddest chick in the literary game.

To my *sheros*: Cindy Adams, Cathy Hughes, Janet Langhart, Suzanne de Passe, Freda Payne, and the late Mary Wilson, thank you for setting such a fine example for Black women.

To my wonderful posse: Rita Ali, Anthony Bowles, Theresa Bowick, Shelley Brooks, Suzette Charles, Jocelyn Coley, L. Marilyn Crawford, Copper Cunningham, Janis DaSilva, Angelo Ellerbee, Patrick Ewing, Irene Gandy, Dawne Marie Grannum, Penny Grant, Karl Allen Griggs, Shannon Hales, James Hester, Sue Ann Henderson, LaToya Jackson, Marva Lee, Adrienne Lopez, Wynton Marsalis, Kenneth McCoy, Kimberly Mercer, Jawn Murray, Johnny Newman, Charles Oakley, Renell Perry, Jean and Martin Shafiroff, Todd and Liz Shapiro, Ethel Stewart, Karina Tatarksi, Phynjuar Thomas, Trent Tucker, Lu Willard, Nathan Hale Williams, and Peter Wise, thank you for always having my back.

To the Ann Arbor Crew, Theresa Campbell and Barbara Jean Patton, we will always be friends for life.

What can I say? I love all my Delta Sigma Theta sorors. A special shout out to my Untouchable 31, Alpha Chapter Howard University line sisters, especially Dr. Patricia Baranco, Dr. Suzanne Randolph, and Judge Sharon Strickland Williams, as well as my special Sandra Hall Morris.

My dear cousins: Josie Anthony, Tijuana Anthony, Susan Anthony, Courtney Benson, Claudette Anthony-Bush, Jackie Johnson Jones, Rev. Shanan Jones, Rev. Jamie Smith, Rev. Conrad Tillard, Mark Winkler, and Attorney Maury Winkler...we are truly family!

This novel is dedicated to the champion of my heart, Michael Spinks, my real-life Royale!

Love,
Flo

PROLOGUE

June 2016
Los Angeles
A Vile Verdict

Sitting between Rome Nyland and Royale Jones, Valerie Rollins held both of their hands tightly as the jury filed into the courtroom to announce Valerian Davidson and Claude Hoskins' fate. The two career criminals were finally going behind bars forever. They were on trial for several murders, numerous thefts, and conspiracies. However, that was only a dream for Val, her longtime love, Royale, as well as her best friend, Rome.

Judge Basil Simpson was presiding.

"Will the foreperson of the jury please stand?" An attractive Black woman, wearing a tan Saint John's pantsuit stood up.

"Have you reached a verdict?" asked Judge Simpson.

"Yes, Your Honor."

Judge Simpson then asked, "Will the defendants please stand?"

Valerian and Claude, whom Val often referred to as the "sons of satan," stood up.

"You may read the verdict."

"Your Honor," said the foreperson. "We find the defendants not guilty!"

"Thank you for your service and time jury. Mr. Hoskins and Mr. Davidson, you are free to go!"

Claude and Valerian hugged each other. Then, Valerian pointed his finger at Royale, and spoke to him in a whisper. "Coming for all of you, cousin!"

Then he and Claude, accompanied by a group of misled followers, pranced out of the courtroom.

The prosecuting attorney approached a stunned Valerie.

"This isn't over, you know. The district attorney and FBI are now preparing a case against them in Sag Harbor, New York as we speak. These charges they just got acquitted on here will all be included in the upcoming case on the east coast."

"Yes, I know. We are cooperating with the New York authorities. I hope it will not take too long for the new case to go to trial," said Rome. "All right. Let's get back to New York before those two have a chance to attack us today."

"It is definitely time to jet back to the east coast and put as much distance as we can between Valerian and Claude for now. Justice will take place eventually. One way or the other, karma is going to catch up with them. When it do, they will pay for all the horror and pain they have inflicted on others," Valerie sighed.

CHAPTER ONE

Summer 2021
Saturday Morning
Sag Harbor
Sincere and Claude

THE HOLY TEMPLE of Mary Magdalene in Sag Harbor, New York, turned into a crime scene as the historically Black town in the Hamptons' local police officers, New York State police, and FBI agents raided the church and its adjacent parsonage. They were all there to arrest Pastor Claude Hoskins and Valerian Davidson, also known as, Sincere, for kidnapping Turquoise Hobson, and murdering NYPD Officer, Roger Lomax, Caressa Shabazz in New York, and Carlton Jamal in Los Angeles.

In the 1940s and 1950s, subdivisions in Sag Harbor Hills, Azurest and Ninevah, collectively known as SANS, became a summer home destination for upper and middle class Black doctors, lawyers, and dentists. When Jim Crow laws left few recreational options for Black-Americans, the founding residents created these unique communities on underdeveloped land at the outskirts of Sag Harbor Village. The summer houses gave Black Americans a place of their own.

Valerian, Claude, and Royale had been coming to Sag Harbor since they moved from Illinois as kids. Using sign language, a communication used between them since they were kids when they didn't want others to know what they were talking about, Sincere told Claude, "Just keep quiet. I do not care who Royale claims gave us up. We have never even met those guys. They were only connected to Rolondo, and he is dead. There is no way these charges are going to stick."

"I hope Rolondo is really dead. We thought Royale was dead for five years, too."

Royale Jones walked into the parsonage with Rome Nyland. The retired baseball player was also their cousin, so he understood their childhood sign language all too well.

"Unfortunately, for you two, I am alive and thriving, but my cousin, Rolondo, is definitely dead. I am suspecting descending into hell as we speak," said Royale.

Claude extended his hand to Rome. Rome ignored Claude's outstretched hand.

"It is always good to see you, Mr. Nyland," said Claude. "But what are you doing here? In fact, why are you here, Royale?"

Royale told him, "I am here because I own this house and church. I invited Rome to come with me. I also need you to hand over the keys to my orange Bugatti Bordeaux that is parked out front. I guess that Rolondo had it shipped here when he escaped out of the courtroom."

"I'm not giving you that car, cousin. Plus, it is not such a good idea for you to be in it," said Claude.

Royale stretched his hand out to him again.

"I'll decide whether driving my car that Rolondo stole is a 'good idea.' The keys right now or we can add grand theft auto to all these petty crimes you're being charged with today."

"All right, all right. Open that drawer. The keys to everything, including the house and the church, are in it. I'm just saying since you haven't driven it in six years. You may not be safe. But you are the smart jock with the University of Michigan Big Ten education. Do whatever pleases you."

Royale opened the drawer Claude pointed to and saw several keyrings.

"See how easy that was, cousin?"

"Valerian, you know I'm here because I have been chasing your ass for two years," said Rome. "I came to gloat, watching all of this law enforcement haul your ass out of here in handcuffs and shackles."

Rome was a NFL Hall of Famer but was now the head of security for Dumas Electronics. The Black owned multi-billion dollar company formerly owned by Victor Dumas, who died after battling colon cancer four years ago.

Rome's phone rang. He picked up right away.

"Hey, Amethyst. How are you, baby? Listen, I am handling a situation right now. I do not think it is a good idea for you to come out to the Hamptons this weekend. It looks like I'm going to be tied up."

When they heard the name Amethyst, Claude and Sincere exchanged looks.

"What's wrong?" asked Amethyst through the phone.

Rome told her, "Royale's cousins, Valerian Davidson and Claude Hoskins, have just been arrested. Since I have been working on this case for a long time, I'm going to have to work with the authorities all weekend here and in Los Angeles."

Amethyst replied, "I would still like to come out and help

Valerie with whatever she needs. She seems so nice. I feel so sorry for her losing Victor so soon after they got married. You know, the same thing happened to me. She's been so nice to me that I think I can be a lot of help to her as she grieves."

"That is actually a very good idea and a kind gesture on your behalf," said Rome. "Okay. I haven't canceled the car service that Val booked for you yet. The driver should be there soon. I will see you later at Val's house."

The look between Sincere and Claude didn't go unnoticed by Royale. He knew those two jerks as well as himself and something was up. I listened while the officers talked.

"Since these crimes cross state lines, the FBI is going to take this over," said Agent Trent Tubbs. "We are going to take these two detainees back to New York City now."

"Royale, will you at least call an attorney for Sincere and me?" asked Claude.

"You have really gone crazy, Claude. I told you earlier today when I spoke to you on the phone that I know you and Sincere were in on Rolondo trying to kill me."

"Fuck you, Royale," said Sincere. "I don't know what you are talking about. We have always been business partners. Why would we want to kill you? I do not need you to get a damn thing for me. I am going to call my son, Vance. He is worth billions and will get me, his real father, the best legal team money can buy."

A multiple Kentucky Derby winner, Vance Dumas was one of the best jockeys in the world, as well as one of the handful of jockeys of color. Vance, his daughter, Valencia, along with Valerie, were the heirs to his father, Victor's twenty-one-billion-dollar fortune. Once his famous horse, Wildn,' Out, aged out of racing, Vance decided to start an all-Black polo team called The Dumas Diamonds Polo Club. It was currently preparing to participate in this year's Monte Carlo Polo Cup in the South of France.

Rome stared Sincere down.

"This is the third time I have heard you refer to Vance as your son, Valerian. What is up with that?"

"What is up with that is Vance is my son, not Victor's. That little geek brother of mine was so lame that he never realized Andrea was only one month pregnant when she told him she was three months along and they had not had sex in three months. The two of us got busy every day. When she married Mr. Billionaire, Andrea bought me a house down the road from the horse farm, which is still my legal residence. She only married Victor because I told her to so I could get the billions that should have gone to me when our father died. It is a shame that she was in the wrong place at the wrong time and had to die."

"Valerian," said Rome. "I am the director of security for Dumas Electronics, so I know everything about the company. Your dad left Victor a little over a million dollars. He took that and built Dumas Electronics from the ground up. I also know that your father left the same amount of money to you and your mother. So cut the crap about Victor's money should have been yours. That is not true, and you, know it is not."

"Enough," said Agent Tubbs. "It is time to get you two out of here. Since it is Saturday, there's really nothing you can do today, Mr. Nyland. Here is my card. Someone from the bureau will get in touch with either you or Mr. Jones with information about the arraignment, which should take place on Monday in New York City at FBI Headquarters."

He continued. "Mr. Jones, you mentioned that you own this property. The CSI team is going to have to totally sweep it for weapons and drugs, which may take a few days. Do you have someplace else you can stay?"

"Yes, I do," said Royale. "I haven't been here for many years. I'm checked into the American Hotel here in Sag Harbor. You can reach me there as soon as your people are done."

"Will do," said Agent Tubbs, as he and six other members of the FBI escorted Pastor Claude and Valerian out the church's parsonage.

The officers handcuffed Claude and Valerian with their hands in front of them. Claude suddenly stopped short, elbowed Agent Tubbs, and leaned toward a lamp on a table. He quickly pulled a small gold-plated handgun out of the lamp, then shot Agent Tubbs in the back, who was in front of him. He turned toward Royale.

"You should have stayed dead, motherfucker!" yelled Claude.

Before he pulled the trigger a second time, Rome kicked Claude's hand, causing the gun to land in one of the state policeman's hands. The policeman yelled into his radio.

"Officer down at the Holy Temple of Mary Magdalene in Sag Harbor. Send a bus fast!" he yelled into the radio, as another officer kneeled to help Tubbs.

After being in ROTC in college, Rome was a medic when he served in the military during Desert Storm war. He sprang into action instead of Royale.

"Strip his shirt and whatever he has on underneath it. Somebody, bring me some towels," Rome instructed. "Our number one priority is to keep him from bleeding out until we can get him to the hospital.

Blood gushed out of Tubbs' back. Rome grabbed the towels that were handed to him and applied pressure to the area the blood was coming from. The bullet hit Tubbs' abdomen.

"Hang in there, man," said Rome, as he kept the towels, and his hand, on the wound.

The sounds of sirens soon roared through the air as EMT workers rushed in to move Tubbs onto a stretcher.

A member of the Sag Harbor police department rushed inside with his gun pulled out, stared sternly at one of his colleagues.

"How did this happen, Chacon? Didn't you guys sweep this place for weapons?"

"Look, man," answered Chacon. "I have known Pastor Claude for years. I am a member of this church. There is no way that he committed these crimes he is accused of. So, no, I did not do a search for weapons. I did just the opposite and ordered my men not to tear the home of a holy man, connected to my church apart."

"We'll talk about this down at the station. Everyone could have been killed because of your carelessness," the officer stated, whose name plate said Weaver.

Tubbs' FBI colleagues handcuffed Pastor Claude and Valerian with their hands behind their backs and flanked them on both sides and in front and back as they were led out.

"Cousins, it is time you stop trying to kill me. Can't you see I'm Lazarus?" Royale laughed.

"Who the fuck is Lazarus?" Valerian sneered.

"Pastor Claude, please enlighten your sinner of a cousin to chapter eleven, Gospel of John, in the Bible," said Royale.

Claude glared at Royale.

"Well, I will tell you both," said Royale. "Lazarus is the biblical Saint, whom Jesus restored life to four days after his death. Just like me, he came back to life. Your street player days are over."

He then turned to Rome.

"Man, I need to stop hanging around you. Is there any day when you're not involved in a fire fight?"

"Since I have been dealing with your sick family of sons of bitches, very few. It is time to go, brother."

As they headed out, Royale glanced around the living room, which was elaborately decorated with red velvet couches, chandeliers, mirrored walls, and a red fox rug to complement the furniture.

"You can tell a pimp lived here, not the pastor that my cousin was pretending to be. Claude really changed this place around when he thought I was dead. Instead of a church parsonage, this room looks like Iceberg Slim is going to pop out and offer us a drink," Rome laughed.

"Do you think Valerian is telling the truth about being Vance's dad instead of Victor?" Rome asked Royale.

"Yes, I do. Andrea also told me a very long time ago that Sincere is Vance's father."

Rome shook his head.

"It was bad enough that Violet turned out to be Vance's wife and cousin. Now she may have been the poor guy's wife and sister. This makes me totally understand why she committed suicide. It is a miracle that she could function with that decadent secret and still thrived as a famous jockey. That kind of magnitude of incest is unheard of. I also see why Violet kept referring to her own daughter, Valencia, as a 'freak' and never wanted to touch the poor baby. I really hate to be the one to lay this kind of bad news on Val and Vance."

Royale jangled the keys in his hand. "Let me help you out with that. I'll follow you over to Val's," Royale said, in my long lost million- dollar whip. It's nice to have my baby back!"

"Okay, let's do it," said Rome as they headed out the door.

"By the way, I see the rumors about you are true," said Royale.

"What rumors?"

"The rumors that you have smoother moves than the late

Kobe Bryant. May he rest in peace. Between knowing how to save Agent Tubbs' life with the towels and pressure on his wound, and kicking the gun out of Claude's hands like you are a ninja, like Little Carl Carlton sang years ago, you are a bad mamma jamma."

"It is time to blow this joint!" Rome said, laughing.

CHAPTER TWO

Amethyst

AFTER SPEAKING WITH ROME, although it was only ten o'clock in the morning, Amethyst Printup poured a shot of Jack Daniel's bourbon. Her hand shook, gulping down the warm liquor quickly. Amethyst was a former Olympic figure skater. She had smooth skin the color of nutmeg. She told people she was a private duty nurse in New York City. Truth be told, her only job was teaching weekly group skating lessons as part of the Figure Skating in Harlem program, which was seasonal. Life had not painted a pretty picture for Amethyst. In fact, it had been pathetically painful.

In 1980, the United States led a boycott for the summer Olympic games in Moscow to protest the late 1979 Soviet invasion of Afghanistan. In total, sixty-five nations refused to participate in the games, while only eighty countries sent athletes to compete.

The disappointment of not being able to skate in the Olympics, a goal she had worked towards since she was four years old, caused Amethyst to spiral into a deep depression. After a night of drinking back-to-back shots of tequila, combined with smoking marijuana, she decided to go skating alone and snuck into the ice rink at UCLA.

"I know I would have won that gold medal," she had told herself back then, as she tied on her skates. "No one alive could have beaten this move!"

With that said, Amethyst decided to combine the triple axel with the quadruple jump, two of the most dangerous and risky moves for any skater. Quadruple jumps, landed successfully, including four full turns in the air. Nobody ever managed to land this jump in a competition.

Miraculously, in her extremely inebriated state, she euphorically made it through the triple axel.

"Yes, I got this," yelled Amethyst back then.

She forged on to the jump. When she jumped high into the air on the first try and turned, her body would not cooperate.

"Arrrrrrgggghhhhh," came the howling scream as she hit the ice hard, breaking her right leg and dislocating her left shoulder at the same time.

Fortunately, the ice cleaner had just arrived to the rink to get it ready for the next day. As soon as he saw Amethyst lying on the ice, he called 911 right away. It took Amethyst six months to heal from her injuries, which resulted in her being out of commission. The doctors prescribed Oxycontin for the intense pain she was in constantly. The pills led to a heroin addiction that took her years of rehab to kick.

Along the way, she met a group of cousins who were drug dealers, pimps, and the most notorious hustlers a woman like her ever met. They quickly pulled her into their web of scandal and deceit by supplying her with drugs. They also put her to work doing so many degrading and derogatory acts she still shuddered thinking about it. Anxious to help others, after she finally got clean, Amethyst took the shorter route and became a licensed practical nurse. The training program only took one year, which was much easier and faster than going back to college for another four years to earn a registered nursing degree. But in the end, she found treating sick people depressing, so she never pursued a nursing career.

Amethyst saw a news report on television the previous night that said Purdue Pharma, the manufacturers of Oxycontin, had agreed to pay a whopping eight billion settlement that would dissolve the company. With all she had gone through with pills, it was a shame the head honchos were not thrown in jail for life.

A young widow, Amethyst, and the famous, Revered Rome Nyland, had become romantically involved four years ago after a chance meeting on a flight from Los Angeles to New York.His former fiancé, Turquoise Hobson, was kidnapped by the same deadly cousin clan she had met in her twenties. She often wondered if Rome was finished with Turquoise because they were still communicating with each other. Rome was everything a woman could want in a man, a rare combination of a genuine, handsome, and rich.

And now, he had innocently told her Claude Hoskins and Valerian Davidson had been arrested.

Hearing those two names made Amethyst yell out. "God, please don't let them come back into my life!"

The ringing of her phone made Amethyst jump so fast, the shot glass dropped out of her hand, shattering as it hit the floor.

"Hello."

"Hey, Amethyst. This is Valerie. How are you?"

"I'm fine. How are you?"

"It's a day-to-day struggle making it without Victor, but I'm hanging in there," Val told her. "Rome told me you are going to be spending the rest of the weekend with us. Since so much went down today with those two goons getting arrested, I thought instead of going out for dinner or having Jonelle cook, I would just call Sylvia's restaurant for some takeout. Since you are right there in Harlem, would you mind stopping by there to get the food? I will call in the order, pay for it, and tell the driver who is picking you up to go in and get it. There is going to be a lot of food because I'm ordering enough so that Vance's polo team can eat with us too."

"Of course, I will pick everything up, Val. I'd be happy to. Do you know what time the car is going to be here? I am already packed and ready to head out to the Hamptons."

"My driver, Raymond, is already in the city picking up a few things from my apartment that I need out here. How about an hour and a half from now? That will give Sylvia time to get the food ready. I will call the restaurant ASAP," Val told Amethyst.

"Okay, I'm looking forward to seeing everyone when I get there. I have never spent much time in the glamorous Hamptons."

"All righty dighty. We are looking forward to seeing you too. Ciao."

"Bye Val," said Amethyst.

It was an unbelievable blessing Amethyst and Rome had run into each other after more than thirty years. They both were graduates of UCLA where he had been a star running back before playing professional football. He was so fine and seemed nice. She remembered watching him practice sprints on the university's track. Aside from football, Rome also excelled at running. Amethyst and Rome were members of the 1980 Olympic team that never made it to Moscow.

Back then, he had a girlfriend, Davida, who was a cheerleader at UCLA. Amethyst heard Rome and Davida had a son together, but never got married. During their college years, he never even glanced at Amethyst. It was amazing after all that time never even speaking to each other, they bonded on the plane and were practically inseparable ever since.

She looked around her living room. The deed to this lovely house on One Hundred Twenty- Seventh Street and Madison Avenue in East Harlem was in someone else's name, a man that was now dead.

"Please, God, don't let him reach out from the grave and take it back from me through Sincere and Claude, causing my past to come back to haunt me," Amethyst prayed aloud.

"I am so ready for this newfound happiness to last forever."

She went to the kitchen to get the broom and dustpan to sweep up the glass. It would be nice if she could just sweep away her sordid history the same way.

CHAPTER THREE

Valerie

Like Beyonce's mother, Tina Knowles Lawson, and beautiful celebrities such as Lynn Whitfield and Beverly Johnson, Valerie Rollins made women in their sixties look forty. Her looks, spirit, and style were ageless. She was the first African American gossip columnist. After four decades in the business, Val was still hard at work daily. Not only after thirty -years, did she still get up before dawn five days a week to do her daily syndicated radio show, "Gossip To Go With Valerie Ro," but she also wrote a weekly column called, "Val Rollins' Celebrity Buzz," and had an online magazine called Blacknoir.nyc. In addition, along with her stepson, Vance, she oversaw her late husband, Victor's, multi-billion dollar company, Dumas Electronics. Dedicated to family, Valerie helped Vance raise her seven-year-old step granddaughter, Valencia. Valencia's mother, Violet, had tragically committed suicide a few years ago.

* * *

Sylvia's restaurant was the first place Val went to eat when she arrived in New York City after graduating from Howard University. The *Queen of Soul Food* was founded by the late legendary Sylvia Woods in 1962. Established in Harlem, Sylvia's was the community's favorite in Harlem. Val put in a call to the restaurant.

"Sylvia's restaurant, how can we help you?"

"This is Valerie Rollins. I want to place a large order that a friend of mine, Amethyst Printup, and my driver, will be picking up."

"Of course, Valerie. How are you?"

"Good, thank you. How is business going?"

"We're hanging in there, trying to move along daily in this pandemic."

"I understand. I will be so glad when this horror story has an ending to it. I am calling to put in an order. I want to give you my credit card and my driver will pick everything up. Is that okay?"

"Of course, what do you want today?" asked the hostess.

"I want to order everything in trays that will feed around twenty people. Give me a tray of fried chicken with legs and thighs, one with wings and breasts, a tray of fried whiting, then smothered pork chops, regular collard greens, potato salad, peas and rice, string beans, black- eyed peas, and white rice with gravy on the side, plus cornbread. If you have a sweet potato pie and a yellow cake, I will take one of each, too." Val then recited her credit card number, enunciating slowly.

"Okay, I have it all," said the hostess. "What time do you want this to be ready?"

"Will an hour give you enough time?"

"More than enough time. Most of this is ready."

"Okay, thank you so much, hon. I should be in the city for a few days next week. I'll drop by then," said Val.

"Sounds good to me. Thank you so much for everything. Bye."

"Bye bye."

The minute Val hung up with Sylvia's, her phone rang again.

"Hey, Eighty-Eight, what's up?"

"There was a shooting over at the Holy Temple of Mary Magdalene about an hour ago," said the voice on the other end of the phone.

"Oh, my God. Rome headed over there earlier. Is he all right?"

"Yes, he's fine. As usual, the modern day Shaft put on his superman cape, and not only tried to save the life of the FBI agent who got hit, but he also managed to karate kick the gun out of Claude Hoskins' hand."

"What do you mean *tried* to save the FBI agent?" asked Val.

"I just got a tip from an old EMT source of mine. The agent did not make it. He went into cardiac arrest the moment they got him to Stony Brook Southampton Hospital. They couldn't bring him back."

At that moment, the inter-house phone rang.

"Hold on a minute Eighty-Eight," said Val, as she pushed the intercom.

"Yes?" It was her butler and security guard, Dwayne.

"Rome just got back and needs to see you right away, Valerie."

"Thank you. Tell him I will be right there and take him into the kitchen. I don't know what he has to eat in the guest house. Lunch is laid out on the table in case he is hungry. From what I have heard about his experience this morning, that man should be starving."

"You got it," said Dwayne.

Val told Eighty-Eight, "That was my security guard, Dwayne. Rome is here. I have to hang up now. I will let him know that the FBI agent is dead. This is terrible. I will hit you back. Good looking out."

Aside from being the director of security for Dumas Electronics, Rome was like Valerie's business partner as well as her brother from another mother. She had met the former football player turned private investigator twenty years ago when they were trying to find out who killed his cousin, Charmaine Sutton, several others and the famous actress, Jennifer Sands. They solved crimes together ever since.

Rome had become very friendly with Royale Jones, like a real life fairytale. The story of her relationship with Royale was one for the books. They were college sweethearts, they had broken up after Valerie suffered a miscarriage. She never saw him again for thirty years until a man, who looked like and claimed to be Royale, surfaced at Mr. Chow's restaurant in Beverly Hills.

Although it had been ages since Val had seen Royale, he was lighter and thinner than he had been when they were in college. Something about him didn't feel right. When he acted like he had never seen her before, Val followed his lead. By then, she and Victor Dumas had fallen in love, so she felt it was best to let her history with Royale stay buried.

Only that Royale turned out to be his lookalike cousin, Rolondo Jemison, who thought he had killed Royale, and assumed his identity. Instead, the real Royale was rescued by some fishermen from Crooked Island, which was an almost desolate place close to the Bahamas. After being shot and hitting his head, he suffered from amnesia and didn't have recollection of who he was or where he came from. The people on the island gave him the name Columbus Isley.

Royale's memory returned five years later after he saw a newspaper article with a photo of Val and Rolondo in it. He flew straight to New York to try to find Rolondo, but instead ran into Valerie. After her husband's death, Valerie and Royale rekindled their friendship, realizing they still had feelings for each other.

The first night she ran into him, Royale told her, "We are still the same two people, and I have never stopped loving you."

Looking around the luxurious surroundings of the bedroom in her two-level master suite, Val was still in awe of this house Victor secretly had built before his death four years ago, and gave to her as a wedding gift. He had paid one-hundred-forty-five million dollars for the twelve bedrooms, twelve bathrooms, thirty-five acre estate, which was the largest ocean frontage in the Hamptons, spanning nearly a quarter mile.

There were also two ponds bordering the property, with views of Mecox Bay and the Atlantic Ocean. Every morning she woke up, Val was astounded by the gated entrance; the three separate wings in the main house, and her staff and guest wing, that also had a separate entrance. For the time being, Rome was staying in the carriage house, which had three bedrooms and one and a half bathroom. Val's living quarters were comprised of a mini mansion onto itself, boasting a living room, dining room, kitchen, two bathrooms, and three bedrooms. For security reasons, she had a private entrance from the outside so no one would know when she entered the main house.

Val took a quick look in the mirror, putting on lipstick and prepared to start the day.

Since Val planned to be at home this Saturday, she dressed casually in Beyoncé's second Ivy Park collection with Adidas. The collab was such a hit that it sold out almost immediately. She had did a story on her radio show that morning for a few lucky ladies who were friends with Queen Bey herself. The superstar songstress sent large, wheeled carts filled with the beautiful garments to Kerry Washington, her mom Tina Knowles Lawson, and other entertainment industry A-listers, who included one of Val's favorite actresses Mo'Nique. The Academy Award winning actress put on an entire fashion show when she opened the box to show off on her Instagram stories.

The mobile closets were covered with a drop screen featuring the same mountain landscape as the Find Your Park campaign, so celebs like Kerry and Miss Tina could have their very own photoshoots from home. That Beyoncé was one class act!

She sprayed on her favorite perfume, Ysatis, by Givenchy and headed out to see Rome.

Like Val predicted, Rome was famished. He sat at the table, helping himself to the luncheon buffet Jonelle put out every day. To her surprise, Royale was with him. Seeing him always sent a warm and fuzzy feeling throughout Val's body. On Saturdays, Val did not like to make her devoted cook prepare food, so just like she was getting dinner from Sylvia's in the city, she told Jonelle to order an assortment of Chinese food from Fusion Express, close to them in East Hampton.

Hugging both men, Val told Rome," I heard you had your usual, almost deadly, exciting morning."

After all these years of collaborating with each other, Val and her sources still never ceased to amaze Rome.

"It was pretty tough, but Valerian is finally on his way to jail along with Claude."

"You should have seen Rome in action. If he hadn't been there, that FBI agent would be dead!" Royale told Val.

Putting some Kung Pao chicken and brown rice on her plate, Val sat down next to Rome.

"I'm afraid I have some bad news for you guys. Agent

Tubbs coded when he got to the hospital. He went into cardiac arrest. He is dead."

Banging his hand on the table, Rome exclaimed, "Damn! Damn! Damn!"

Royale shook his head.

"Look, Val, I hate to be the bearer of more bad news. Is Vance here?"

"No, he's at his house. Do you need to talk to him about something?"

"This morning, Valerian insisted that Vance is his son. This is the third time he's said so," Rome told her. "Royale thinks it could be true."

"Really?" Valerie asked, looking at Rome.

"Unfortunately, I know it's true. His mother, Andrea, told me Sincere is his father, not Victor, when Vance was a baby. Violet always knew that she and Vance had the same father. I don't know why she went along with Valerian's sinister plot and married Vance, then proceeded to have Valencia with her own brother as the father. She was so twisted just like her father and mother, Betty Lum. Where is Valencia?"

"She's out in the stables with Esperanza," said Val. "She's a true combination of Violet and Vance. At seven -years-old, Valencia is more comfortable around horses than people. I think we need to head over to Vance's house right now to give him this awful news immediately. I hope this information does not put him over the edge. First, his wife was his half- cousin. Now, she may be his half- sister, making Valencia his niece and daughter. To top it off, he lost his father after not knowing Victor had cancer. This is some sick shit. What kind of woman was Andrea? To think she was one of my idols ever since she made history when she became the first Black full-figured model to walk runways globally back in the seventies."

"Andrea was always a sociopath. She was constantly

looking for the next score, finding a mark to get money out of. Victor was that mark. Millions of dollars was not enough for her. She had to have billions," Royale said.

"Getting this awful news about Vance's possible paternity sends chills through my body. It is as if Andrea is still looking to score, as if she's reaching out to hurt Vance from her grave," Val said.

CHAPTER FOUR

Vance

"Damn, Vance, you may be short, but your dick is bigger than Andre the Giant," said Sapphire, a bronze beauty with dazzling dark brown eyes, whom the playboy polo player had hired to move in with him for the rest of the spring and summer. Having a sensual trio at his beck and call twenty-four-seven, meant Vance didn't have to search for women, servants, or sex. He just had to lay back and ride his horse.

As Sapphire pleasured him orally, his other two live-in ladies of the night, her identical twin sister, Saffron, and Ashro, an Asian call girl, were busy making love to each other as they swung up and down his stripper pole.

Most guys had man caves, but Vance installed an erotic suite in his eighty-five million dollars East Hampton mansion. Patterned after a five thousand dollars per night room with a stripper pole in it at the Palms Hotel in Las Vegas, this special space where he spent most of his time, boasted an eight- foot round rotating bed and mirrored ceiling, an extra- large shower that could fit five people in it, a Jacuzzi, a full bar that he sometimes hired naked women to bartend, a movie theater sized television and Creston controlled black drapes that wrapped around the room. The exquisite surroundings were decorated in purple and black with a hint of beige. All the girls' lingerie was custom made and the same color by La Perla. Vance had met them one night while hanging out at Treasures Gentlemen's Club & Steakhouse in Las Vegas, an upscale adult club with a tantalizing choice of women. After three terrible relationships, one of which his wife, Violet, turned out to be a con woman. Not only had he been a set-up his entire life, but she also turned out to be his cousin. Vance was done with commitment. That night in Las Vegas, and being entertained and erotically satisfied by these three women, he offered them two hundred and fifty thousand dollars apiece to spend the polo season with him in the Hamptons. Sex was Vance's drug of choice. Now, the only time his dick wasn't hard was either when he was cumming or riding his horse, Wild n' Out.

After Sapphire finished deep throating him, he lied down at the bottom of the stripper pole, where Ashro and Saffron landed on top of him, grinding away.

"Fuck it, life can't get any better than this!" yelled Vance.

"The bell on your gate is ringing," said Ashro.

"See who it is," Vance told her breathlessly.

She pushed the button on the phone for the gate.

"Hello."

"Hi. This is Valerie Rollins for Vance. Can you tell him I am here with Rome Nyland and Royale Jones? It's urgent that we speak with him."

Vance grabbed the phone out of Ashro's hand.

"Hey, Val. Drive on in. I'll be right there."

After putting on a pair of sweatpants and a matching tee shirt, Vance slipped on a pair of Gucci slippers. "All right, my loves. We will pick this back up later. My stepmother is here to see me about something. Put on your regular maids' uniforms and come down to fix everyone some cocktails," he told the girls.

Sapphire slowly caressed Vance's manhood through his pants.

"We'll never be able to thank you for changing our lives forever."

Fondling her nipple, Vance told her, "No problem, baby. I promised I would take you from the pole to a palatial palace."

Vance bounded down the spiral staircase before Val asked him what he had been doing and opened the door.

"Welcome to Dumas Playhouse," said Vance as he bowed. "Come right this way."

The room was beautifully decorated with a gray and black, quilted satin couch on four silver legs, with matching huge and plush chairs. There was a huge chandelier hanging from the ceiling. A gray rug woven with black and beige spirals was in the middle of the floor. There were paintings of horses flanking the walls, with a life-sized portrait of Vance and his horse as a centerpiece. The base of the coffee table was a horse's head.

Valerie said, "Your decor is so beautiful, Vance. You have done an incredible job on your first home as a bachelor."

"Thank you, Val. That means so much coming from you, a lady who has impeccable taste."

Saffron, Sapphire, and Ashro walked into the living room with matching black mini dresses, and white laced aprons monogrammed with a huge "D" for Dumas. Black, five-inch Christian Louboutin heels completed their looks.

Val did all she could do to keep her composure and not burst out laughing. Royale and Rome's eyes almost popped out of their sockets.

"Can we get you all something to drink?" they asked in unison.

"It's a little early, but in honor of being in Vance's new home, I'll have a glass of chardonnay," answered Val. "Kendall Jackson, if you have it."

"We do. Vance ordered several cases for whenever you visit, Miss Valerie," answered Ashro.

"And what can we get for you two gentlemen?" Saffron asked seductively.

"Water is fine for me," Rome told her. The consummate retired athlete had never indulged in alcohol.

"I guess I'll join Val and also have a glass of wine," said Royale.

Vance's living room had a full bar. It only took them a few minutes to serve the drinks. Ashro set a bottle of Kendall Jackson in a sterling silver bucket on the table and then stood back.

"Thank you," said Val.

For a woman who ran her mouth nonstop for a living, Valerie was uncharacteristically quiet. Rome and Royale were also more mellow than usual, which caused Vance to realize the three of them had come to his home unannounced to discuss something that must be very serious.

He spoke to the girls.

"Okay ladies, you can head back to the kitchen. I'll call you when I need you."

Rome could not contain himself anymore.

"My man, Vance. I don't even want to know what agency you hire your maids from, but you have outdone yourself this time, my brother."

Laughing, Vance slapped Rome five. "Brother, nothing beats unattached built-in round-the clock pussy!"

Even though she had some very sobering news for her stepson, Val laughed uncontrollably.

"I don't even want to know what their real duties are! No wonder you didn't want to stay on my property with the rest of your polo team."

"It's nice to see all three of you, but I know you didn't come over here out of the clear blue sky in the middle of the afternoon to discuss my staff. What are you guys really here for? Is Valencia all right?" asked Vance.

Valerie took the lead.

"Of course, she's fine. We have some other not great news for you. Sweetheart, this morning Your Uncle Valerian and your cousin, Claude Hoskins, were arrested for a laundry list of charges. In the process, Claude shot and murdered an FBI agent. "

"In usual Sincere fashion, he cursed me out. Then he said he was going to call you to get him a lawyer," said Royale.

"Why would Uncle Valerian say that? He has got to know that I would never help him the way he set up my father and tried to kill him for years," said Vance.

"Sincere then went on to say that he is your father, not your uncle," explained Royale. "Vance, I hate to lay this heavy stuff on you, but for the first time in Sincere's life, I think he may be telling the truth. Your mother was pretty doped up on a regular basis, so at the time, I really didn't believe her. But she told me that Sincere was your biological dad shortly after you were born, which would in reality make Victor your uncle."

Although he rarely drank alcohol, Vance stood up, walked over to the bar, and poured himself a full glass of Hennessy, then took a long sip.

Staring at Royale, he asked, "So cousin, whom I am so happy entered my life, you are saying that my wife, Violet, who committed suicide, was my half -sister, which makes Valencia my daughter and my niece?"

"It is a good possibility," answered Royale.

Speechless, Vance sat down next to Val. He then stood up, poured himself another glass of cognac, then threw it against the wall.

As Rome jumped up to restrain him, Val threw her arms around him.

"I wish I could kill both of those lowdown, cock sucking bitches; my mother and my dead wife again. Hell, I should even order a hit on my ex-wife, Roshonda, who used to date my mother. They are all pieces of shit who are cut from the same cloth. They aren't even human!" yelled Vance.

Hearing all the commotion and yelling, sent the girls, as well as Kwami, Vance's valet and main bodyguard, running into the living room.

"What's happening in here, boss?" asked Kwami.

Vance crumbled to the floor with Val's arms still around him and remained silent.

"Why don't you and these lovely ladies get the rest of the staff to clean this glass and liquid up? The three of us will make sure that Vance is all right," Royale told Kwami.

"Is that okay with you, boss?" asked Kwami.

Still speechless, Vance simply nodded yes.

"Fine. Boss, why don't you lead them into your study while we tidy up in here? Follow me, ladies. I'll get the cleaning staff."

Vance managed to stand up. The ringing of Royale's phone broke the eerie silence that had engulfed the room.

"Hello."

"This is Sincere, cousin."

Royale put the phone on speaker so everyone could hear what was going on.

"I know you are not wasting your one phone call on me

because I already told you and Claude that I am not going to help you. I meant what I said earlier."

"Just give me Vance's number."

"I'm right here, Valerian," said Vance. "What do you want?"

"Since you are with this clown, I assume by now that he has told you that I am your father, not that simpering wimp of a dead brother of mine."

"First of all, if you ever disrespect my father like that again, I will kill you. He didn't even know you existed until Val discovered a photo of my mom and you and noticed your resemblance to my dad. Then you held a gun to him at the Cash Call Futurity Race in Los Angeles seven years ago. I bet you were shocked when you found out he was a black belt in karate and took you and your weapon down. To answer your question, yes, I just heard this ridiculous rumor, but I don't believe you," Vance told him.

"You had better believe it! I am currently at the FBI head-quarters in New York City, but I will probably be released from here very soon. Line up one of your fancy doctors so that we can get DNA tests. You will see that I am telling the truth. And don't try anything funny. I have had people watching you for your entire thirty-seven years on this earth. I will see you sooner than you think, my son. Goodbye."

"Vance, you don't have to pay him any attention," said Val.

"No, I am going to find out if this is true. Now I realize why Violet would never touch Valencia, and kept calling her a 'little freak.' Can you contact a DNA expert to meet with me, Val?"

"Yes, I will take care of it. I wonder what Valerian meant when he said that he won't be in custody much longer. I am going to get on the horn right away to find out. For now, why not come over to my house to have dinner this evening with the guys on your polo team. I ordered a bunch of food from Sylvia's that Amethyst is bringing out from the city, and I feel it would be good for you to see your daughter. This lineage catastrophe is not her fault. She needs your love, Vance."

Although he was normally a tough and hard as nails grown man, Vance started crying. In a matter of minutes, the fearless Kentucky Derby winning jockey was once again just a puny kid, whose only refuge from his mother's abuse had always been horses.

He stood up, then asked Royale, "Do you mind staying here with me until then? Even though I have security, I will feel safer with you around. Val is right. I need to see my child as well as show my polo team some leadership."

"Of course, I will, little cuz. Can I speak to you for a minute before you leave Valerie? I'll walk you out."

"Yes, you can." Giving Vance a hug, Val told him, "We will see you in a couple of hours. Feel free to bring your sexy trio and let Kwami know he is also welcome to come in and eat. I will have everything taken care of with the DNA analyst by the time you get to the house. Rome, can you do a sweep of Vance's house while Royale and I talk?"

"You got it."

Royale followed Val outside to Vance's circular driveway. Not able to resist, he lightly kissed her.

"Royale, I thought that we decided it's too soon after Victor's death for us to be physically involved."

He silenced her words with a deep kiss.

"Victor has been dead for nearly four years, Valerie. I am not down with putting our happiness on hold any longer. There is too much going on, five hundred thousand lives lost due to the pandemic. Not to mention, all this tragedy that will not seem to go away. Tomorrow is not promised to us anymore. Our lives can be cut short in the bat of an eyelash. I do not want to waste another day without you by my side. Plus, I also need your help with my minor league baseball team. I was extremely impressed with the way you put together the press conference for the Dumas Diamonds Polo Club and would love it if you could do the same thing for the Sag Harbor Scorpions. Can I steal you away tonight for an after dinner drink so that we can discuss you helping me out?"

"All right. That's a great name for your team. Have you found a stadium for them to play in?"

"Yes, I'm looking into using the Mitchell Athletic Complex in Freeport, Long Island."

Their conversation was interrupted by the beeping of Val's phone.

Holding up the phone so that Royale could also read the text message, Val told him, "This is a text from my friend, Herelema Owens."

The text read, *I have a source down at the FBI Headquarters in Manhattan. The case against Valerian Davidson did not even go to arraignment. The charges have been dropped because there is no proof that he knew any of the victims. He is walking out of there now.*

"This nightmare just won't end," said Val. "Please tell Rome to hurry. We have to alert our security company to send over more guys to the house. We can have a drink in my suite at the house after dinner. I won't be able to go anywhere." Royale gave her one more quick kiss before heading back inside to alert Rome.

Meanwhile, in Vance's kitchen, Saffron, Sapphire, and Ashro were in a three-way text with each other so their conversation wasn't heard. When they met Vance in Las Vegas, it wasn't an accident. Their pimp, Sincere, had paid one of the new members of Vance's polo team, Jamal Warren, who was extremely envious of his boss, to carefully orchestrate the ladies' introduction to Vance.

"*Did you hear the man who looks just like Rolondo say that Paster Claude and Sincere had been arrested? Vance called him Royale.*"

"*Yes, he also said that he's their cousin, and Vance's.*"

"*The question is, what do we do now?*"

The most conniving of the exotic dancer's trio, Ashro, answered. "*We stick with the plan of embezzling all of Vance's billions, then hightailing it out of the country. The way I see it, with Pastor Claude and Sincere locked up and Rolondo dead, the entire take will be ours.*"

Sapphire chimed in. "*Do you think Royale is working with his cousins?*"

"*It didn't sound like it. He seems to be on Rome Nyland and Valerie Rollins' team. Let's just lay back and see if he says anything to us. Also remember, Rolondo always told us some woman named Amethyst used to be his bottom bitch. And we can always stay in her house somewhere in Harlem that he owned. I have her number in my phone just in case we need a back-up plan,*" said Saffron.

"*All right. Let's just keep Vance sexually satisfied. It probably wouldn't be a bad idea to also get in Rome and Royale's pants. I hear they are both wealthy guys, and they may be old, but those two men are fine as wine in the summertime. Who knows? Hooking up with them could bring in a few more million bucks,*" said Ashro.

She opened her arms wide and looked up at the kitchen's high ceiling.

"*Then soon the three of us can live like this on a regular basis. Won't that be grand?*"

CHAPTER FIVE

Saturday evening
Mayhem on the Menu

WITH ALL THE craziness that went down in the morning, the day passed quickly. Before Valerie knew it, Amethyst arrived with the food, and they were both helping Jonelle and the rest of her staff heat things up and place everything into serving dishes in the property's original greenhouse, which Val had transformed into an outdoor dining room with electric heaters attached to it. Knowing what a huge fan Val was of Mackenzie-Childs' home goods and furniture, Victor had furnished it just like the Mackenzie-Childs' Indigo Villa. Everything from the tables, chairs, the tablecloths, plates, and silverware were covered in the famous black and white checks. Even Val matched her surroundings, blending into the decor, wearing a winter white sweater dress, accentuated with a Mackenzie-Childs' scarf and black and white Christian Louboutin boots.

"Your home is so beautiful, Val," Amethyst complimented.

"I have Victor to thank for being able to live like royalty.

The man was psychic. Who would have imagined just one year ago that there was going to be a coronavirus pandemic? Thank God we have this outside dining room. Otherwise, early in the pandemic, I would not have been able to have more than eight people sit down for dinner. And after all the bad news that we have been hit with today, we all need to be together in a loving atmosphere tonight."

"I'm so glad you feel that way, Miss Valerie."

Startled by the voice behind the words, Val turned around to see Turquoise, Rome's former fiancé. She was standing right behind her, wearing a Chanel face mask.

"How did you get in here?"

Turquoise smirked and held up the two bottles of Jay-Z's Armand de Brignac, Ace of Spades Champagne she was carrying.

"I'm here to deliver this expensive bottle of champagne. I knew exactly how to get here because I contacted the real estate agent out here for Victor when he decided to buy you this grand compound. To my misfortune, we all know that I have been in a detox program for a long time and your husband died, but I still had the address and got a big piece of the commission. I just sailed right through the gate behind the liquor delivery van."

"What do you want, Turquoise?" asked Rome, as he entered the green house. "I thought you were back in Los Angeles."

"I want you back, baby. So, I decided to fly back to New York, then rented a car and drove straight out here to Bridge-hampton to ask Valerie where I could find you. And here you are, up under her fat ass as usual."

"I see your residence in an institution failed to improve your nasty ways, Turquoise. And by the way, I didn't order this champagne," said Val.

Amethyst stood there quietly, watching the scenario unfold. Before she could figure out how to react, Royale strolled into the backyard. He drove his Bugatti over instead of riding in Vance's limousine. She had met him last year while having dinner with Val and Rome at Jean Georges' restaurant in Manhattan, but he was such a dead ringer for Rolondo, whom had been the most dangerous man amongst Sincere and Claude. Looking at Royale shot chills through her body. Not wanting to give her connection to his cousins away, she kept her composure, but frightfully froze in her seat.

Turquoise knew Rolondo as Royale Jones. She had never met the real Royale, so she thought he was Rolondo, who she had an affair with while she was engaged to Rome.

Turquoise took one look at Royale, then screamed as she fainted.

Rome picked Turquoise up, and Val grabbed a cloth napkin filled it with ice, then handed it to him. Putting the cold cloth on the back of her neck, he laid Turquoise down on one of the lounge chairs and felt her neck for a pulse.

"She's fine," said Rome. "Come on back, sweetheart. That is not Rolondo. This is Royale, his cousin, whom he was impersonating."

Although Turquoise opened her eyes, she looked like she was shell shocked.

Noting Rome still referred to his ex-fiancé as sweetheart, Val said, "Take her up to one of the guest suites, Rome," said Val. "I can't kick her out in the shape she's in. Let her rest for a while."

"I'm sorry about all this, Doll. I'll be right back down," Rome said, turning to Amethyst. He got Turquoise on her feet and slowly walked her out as she still looked at Royale like he was a ghost.

Val touched Amethyst's hand.

"I'm also sorry that Turquoise showed up like this," said Val. "As you can see, there is no love lost between that woman and me. By the way, this is my, friend Royale Jones. You two met last year, remember?"

"Of course, I remember him. I could never forget a handsome man like you." Amethyst smiled at Royale, thinking if things with Rome did not work out, he would be the perfect rebound guy.

Although he was a retired Major League baseball player; he had the height of a basketball player. Just like Rolondo had been, this man happened to be Rick Fox type of fine, with skin the color of honey, green eyes, and wild curly salt and pepper gray hair. He was the type of guy she always fell for. Those movie star looks were precisely why she was taken with Rolondo, allowing him to lead her down the slippery slope of drugs to disaster. They could have easily been mistaken for identical twins instead of cousins. "I watched you play baseball for years and have always been a huge fan."

"The same here. I always enjoyed seeing your graceful moves on the ice."

He then took Val's hand in his.

"There is never a dull moment around you. I feel like I am living in the middle of an action movie. I thought we had enough tragedy for one day, starting with the murder of the FBI agent this morning, Claude and Sincere getting locked up, Vance's new situation, and now Rome's former fiancé pops up," said Royale. "So that is the infamous Turquoise who was banging Rolondo behind Rome's back after that bastard left me for dead and stole my identity?"

"That is the devious Miss Hobson in the flesh," laughed Val. "I can't believe she had the audacity to show up here tonight. What would you like to drink?"

"Water is fine. I had better keep a clear head. You never

know what additional mayhem may be included on your menu."

With old school Motown music playing in the background, three bartenders stood with water, chardonnay, merlot, and champagne on their trays. One of them held out the tray with water in Mackenzie-Childs' goblets to Royale. Stevie Wonder's "Living for the City" started playing. Not taking the drink offered to him, Royale grabbed Val's hand and twirled her around to the music.

"I remember how you used to love this song when we were in college."

"I still love it," said Val. "I actually did a story about Stevie Wonder on the radio yesterday. He recently told Oprah Winfrey that he is moving to Ghana indefinitely as part of his efforts to shield his lineage of grandchildren and great grand-children from racial injustice in the United States. If your cousin, Valerian, keeps messing with us, we should join Stevie."

"All right, all right, let's get this party started," said Vance, as he made a grand entrance with Saffron, Sapphire, Ashro, and Kwami, along with three members of the Dumas Diamonds polo team, Jamal Warren, Nino Lopez, and Lee Iger. The guys and everyone who lived on the estate were tested weekly for Coronavirus and vaccinated, so while they were on the property, masks were not necessary. "I see the champagne arrived."

Grateful that Vance seemed to have recovered from the horrific news about his own lineage earlier in the day, Val hugged him tightly.

"Thank you. Now I know where the bubbly came from."

"The Ace of Spades is to toast my man, Jay-Z, on that huge deal he made for the champagne. Jay recently pocketed three hundred million dollars by selling fifty percent of Armand de Brignac to LVMH's Moet Hennessy. Then later in the week, according to Forbes.com, the mega-deal maker sold a significant majority stake in Tidal; his music and entertainment streaming platform to Square for two hundred and ninety-seven million dollars. And, to think I ran into him and Jack Dorsey, who is the CEO of both Twitter and Square, just walking down the street not far from here last summer. Now I know what they were cooking up," said Vance.

"I know," said Val. "I did a story on the radio on both of the mergers. You arrived right on time. Here comes your baby girl!"

Almost knocking her father down, Valencia jumped into Vance's arms.

"Daddy. Daddy. Ga-Ga said you were coming," she said, kissing his face.

"Hey, Sweetie Pie, "said Vance as he swung her around.

Always a flirt, Nino kissed Val on the cheek.

"You look beautiful as usual, Valerie."

"And as usual, you will always be the Chocolate Casanova," Val laughed. "Guys, get a drink, grab a plate and help yourself to the food."

Jamal and Sapphire were seeing each other under the radar. Also, a jockey turned polo player, Jamal, had grown up with Vance in Kentucky. Vance's father funded a horse riding school for underserved Black youth in the area, and Jamal enrolled in the program at the age of ten. He even lived in a dormitory on Dumas Farms until he graduated from high school. He then started to professionally ride horses as well as work for the Dumas family. Although he had grown up with Vance, Jamal had always resented Vance was born into tremendous wealth.

While there, he developed a close relationship with Vance's mother. Coupled with envy, this resentment turned to bloodlust. It was worse now since Vance had bought his woman. However, he knew what he was getting into when he became involved with an exotic and ambitious woman such as Sapphire. She was too fine for him to let go of, so he bit the bullet and let her do her thing. He would get even with Vance one day. As soon as he walked into the backyard, he was by her side in a flash.

Kissing the trio of sex pots on their cheeks, Jamal told Sapphire, "You look especially lovely today. What did Vance do, buy out Gucci for you ladies?"

All three of them dressed in Gucci head to toe. Sapphire and Saffron dressed alike in blue Gucci short sleeve knit wool blend dresses with matching shoes, while Ashro was clad in a Gucci red with a web Viscose Jersey dress and matching shoes.

"Practically," said Sapphire. "We took a trip into Harlem to Dapper Dan's brownstone and Vance let us pick out whatever we liked, including purses."

"I love Dapper Dan," chimed in Val. "I am so proud that he launched a fashion line with Gucci two years ago. Back in 1993, I was afraid that I was the reason his store, Dapper Dan's Boutique, closed."

"Why did you think that, Val?" asked Royale, helping himself to a plate and sat down next to her.

"Mike Tyson got into a fight with a contender named Mitch Green at the shop one night. The next day, I went up there to do a story on it for the New York Post. Not realizing the seriousness of it, I wrote about all the bolts of Gucci, Louis Vuitton, and Fendi's fabric that was there. Back then, he made custom clothes for all the celebrities. The day after the story ran, the Feds closed him down. I was so upset over what I had unintentionally done."

"And you lived to tell this story," Vance joked.

"Two years ago, Dapper Dan and I did a book signing together at Sylvia's and he told me they were constantly closing him down all the time anyway, so it was not my fault," said Val.

"Anyway, it's all roses now for him. Dap is included in Time Magazine's 100 Most Influential People of 2020 issue. That is fabulous."

Rome came rushing back, yelling. "Dwayne, round up the rest of the security. We have a problem."

"What is it now, Rome?" asked Val.

"Valerian is at the gate."

"Let him come in," said Vance.

"Are you serious?" Val asked him.

"As a heart attack. I need to speak to him face-to-face. Let him in."

"Okay, Vance. This is your home, too. Esperanza, take Valencia and her security to the nursery. Lock the door and don't come out until Rome let you know that it is okay."

"Yes, Miss Valerie," Esperanza said, taking Valencia's hand, and leaving the greenhouse.

Vance kissed Valencia on her forehead.

"I'll come up and see you soon, baby.

Rome told the gate security on his walkie talkie to escort Valerian to the back.

Visibly shaking at the thought of coming into direct contact with Sincere after so many years, Amethyst told Rome, "Baby, this is all a little too much drama for me. I think I'll go to your house and finish eating there."

The twins and Ashro were also on edge, not having any idea if Sincere was going to give their real purpose for being with Vance up or what he was going to do or say.

"Miss Valerie, can we have the waiters grab some food and wine for us too, so we can keep Amethyst company? This sounds like there should just be family out here," asked Ashro.

"We are all family," said Valerian as he strutted in as if he owned the compound, instead of being the outcast that he was. "I have nothing to hide."

Looking at the three girls, and then staring down Amethyst, Valerian continued. "Vance, my son, you are a chip off the old block. You make a habit of surrounding yourself with beautiful women, just like I do. Like father, like son."

"Like I told you earlier, I am not your son!" Vance yelled as he picked up a steak knife from the table and plunged it into Valerian's chest.

CHAPTER SIX

The Party is Over
Sincere/Valerian

As Royale and Rome wrestled the knife from Vance's hand, Valerian sat up laughing.

"You are one stupid little fool," he told Vance. "Do you think I would come over here among all of you Shaft wannabes without some protection? I have on a multi-threat vest that can stop a bullet or a blade."

Kissing Amethyst on her lips, Rome said, "Baby, why don't you take Vance's three friends, Nino, Jamal, and Lee out back to my house? Jonelle, can you have the staff pack up food and some drinks for them? Then you all just stay with them and enjoy yourselves."

Jonelle grabbed an empty Mackenzie-Childs serving cart and put a few trays on it and beckoned one of the waiters to join her.

Valerian stared at the four ladies as if he could eat them alive as they exited.

"What a shame these beauties have to leave. I was relishing having them for some decadent dessert."

"The day you come near my woman is the day I will finally get rid of you," said Rome. "I can't believe the Feds let you go. Now, please tell us what you want other than Vance's DNA, then get the hell out of here."

"You are more stupid than I thought, Rome. You better watch your latest piece of ass before she skates right out of your life into mine," said Valerian.

Still holding onto Vance, Rome ignored Valerian.

"Sincere, why don't you just leave these people alone?" asked Royale. "It's time for you to throw in the towel. Rolondo is dead. The Feds may not have been able to connect you to any of those crimes, but Claude's handprints are all over them. He's not going anywhere soon, so your little cousin crew of Bugatti Blades that has wreaked havoc from coast-to-coast for more than thirty years is null and void."

"Look, Valerian, I checked with someone at DNA Experts LLC, which is a leading company in Forensic Toxicology," said Val. "I was told that since you are Victor's half-brother, there is a good chance your DNA will match Vance's regardless, so you can stop that charade. A DNA test will prove nothing. But I'm sure you already know that."

"You always thought you were so smart, Valerie. I did not come here for DNA. I never wanted a daughter and I sure as hell have no use for a short piece of shit son like you, Vance. Miss Prissy Valerie, I came here to put you and this polo playing pussy hound on notice that I still want half of Dumas Electronics twenty-one billion dollars fortune," said Valerian.

He then pointed his finger at Royale.

"Dear cousin, you are not off the hook either. You had better not sleep on me. One way or another, I will get my hands on that billion dollars you have buried in silver and gold. The

Bugatti Blades still reign supreme and my cousin crew does, too. Your sorry ass is still alive and so is Rafael. In fact, he became a lawyer while he was in prison and has been released. I am expecting him here in the Hamptons tomorrow to help with Claude's case. And we all know you also like to delve into the fast lane from time to time. I bet your precious Valerie does not realize that you have been in the life too. Watch your back, my peeps. They call me Sincere because I always follow through on my threats. Enjoy your dessert!"

With those words, Valerian picked up the sweet potato pie, flung it at Royale, barely missing him, then strutted out of the yard.

Valerie put both of her arms around Vance and held him close.

"Every time we encounter Valerian, he drains the life out of me. Before Victor died, he told me he thanked God every day that he didn't grow up with that devil because he wouldn't have survived puberty. He was right because dinner didn't even survive once he strutted in here."

Trying to lighten the mood, Royale said, "Yeah, he sure knows how to ruin a party. I was really looking forward to a slice of that pie."

Even Vance laughed, then asked Royale, "Who is Rafael? Please do not tell me I have another wicked cousin or uncle out there."

"I wish you didn't, but Rafael is Rolondo's younger brother. Unfortunately, he also looks very similar to Rolondo and me. He was incarcerated in Illinois when he was seventeen years old for premeditated murder. He is in his early fifties now, so it does not surprise me that he's been released. What does surprise me is that he stayed in touch with Sincere because he and Rolondo totally set Rafael up to take the fall for that murder. Before I got amnesia, I was sending money to the prison to put on his account. I encouraged him to take the college courses and better himself while he was locked up. Maybe becoming a lawyer means that Rafael is rehabilitated from his criminal way of thinking."

Val took Royale's hand in hers.

"How did you turn out to be so nice when the rest of your family is so horrible, darling?"

Caressing her face, Royale told Val, "I haven't always been so nice, baby girl. Sincere is telling the truth. I financed some of their shady deals to make extra money, but I stopped doing it. That is anotherreason Rolondo tried to kill me. But the worst thing I ever did was letting you get away."

Not sure of how he felt about Val rekindling her long ago romance with Royale, Rome kissed her on the cheek and said, "Come on, Vance, let's go get your girls, so you can take them home. This has been far too long of a day. It is time for it to come to an end. Goodnight, Val. I will see you tomorrow. Are you leaving now too, Royale?"

"No, I'm going to stay and talk to Valerie for a bit before I head back to the American Hotel. And Vance, try not to stab anyone tonight or bust up anymore glasses."

"You got jokes, cousin. You got jokes!"

Picking up a plate, for the first time all evening, Val sat down at the table and put food on her plate, then took a sip of wine.

"Grab a plate, Royale. We haven't had a chance to eat all night."

Putting his arms around her, and kissing Val passionately, Royale said, "I would rather grab you. Come on, baby. It has been over three decades. Give this brother a chance."

Val put down her wine glass, kissing him back.

"I always knew you were nothing but a lowdown slut,

Valerie," said Turquoise, as she walked back into the green-house. "Royale, they told me you were dead!"

"Didn't you hear anything Rome said to you earlier? This is the real Royale Jones. That gangster you were sleeping with was an imposter whose name was Rolondo Jemison, and he is dead!"

"Really?" asked Turquoise.

"Yes," said Royale.

"It is very true," said Val as she kissed him again. "Turquoise, since you seem to have recovered, it is time for you to leave my property. You can go peacefully or I can have you thrown out. "

Turning to one of her security guards, who was standing discreetly nearby, Val said, "Kahari, please escort Miss Hobson from the compound."

Taking Turquoise by the arm, Kahari told her, "It's time to go, Miss Hobson."

"But I still haven't had a chance to talk to Rome," said Turquoise.

"I'll tell him to call you," said Val.

As Turquoise was led out, Val whispered to Royale. "It is time to make this a private dinner soiree, baby. We can have it on my side of the house. Jonelle, have the staff bring some trays up to my suite, then take the rest of the night off. I'll see you tomorrow."

Winking at her boss, Jonelle answered, "You got it, Miss Val!"

CHAPTER SEVEN

Valerie and Royale
Bedtime Stories

Val led Royale into her bedroom and locked the door the minute they were inside.

Lifting Royale's knitted polo shirt over his head, she told him, "My head says this isn't right, but my vagina says differently. I am tingling like we're back in Ann Arbor after you hit that homerun for me when I was only nineteen years old. Make love to me, baby. Now!"

As he lightly pushed her down on the bed, Royale whispered, "I've been waiting to hear those words come out of your mouth since I cornered you in the bathroom at the Ritz Carlton last year."

Although they were no longer teenagers, sex between Royale and Valerie was like riding a bicycle. Once you learned how, you never forget. As they undressed each other, their bodies went back in time. Royale hungrily devoured Val's breasts as she reached for his penis, guiding him inside of her.

At sixty-four years old, he was harder than a steel boulder, pounding into her with the energy of a teenager losing his virginity. Meshing their bodies together stroke by stroke, as they reached orgasms simultaneously, Val let out a slow moan that evolved into a satisfied scream!

Laughing, Royale told her, "You better quiet down, sweetheart. Your security staff is going to think I am hurting you! However, you do give new meaning to Cardi B and Megan Thee Stallion's hit *WAP!*"

"I could have told you that before we walked into this bedroom. And my staff would be correct. You did put a hurting on me! I need to stop trying to fool myself or ignore my feelings. I love you so much, Royale. I have to admit I never stopped."

Easing out of Valerie, Royale picked up her left hand, fingering her wedding ring.

"I know Victor has only been dead four years, but why don't you swap his ring for mine? Like I said earlier, I do not want to waste any more time. Will you marry me, Sweet Val?"

Val sat up slowly, then pulled a piece of paper out of her nightstand she had been keeping there since Victor's death.

"I know Vance told you Victor gave his attorney this letter to give to me at the reading of his will. I want you to know what it says."

"Yes, Vance mentioned the letter to me, and I have always wanted to see exactly what Victor thought about our past relationship. Please go ahead and lay it on me."

My Dearest Valerie,

Do not mourn for me. Without your love, my life would not have lasted as long as it did. I have only one request for you. Royale is a good man. Give love a second chance. I will see you when we meet in another lifetime. I love you with all my heart.

Victor.

Val cradled Royale's face in her hands, kissing him passionately. "I guess I had better honor his final request. So, yes, my love, yes. I will marry you."

Royale took off the diamond miniature baseball bat that rarely left his neck and unscrewed it.

Digging deep down into the bottom of the medallion, he pulled out a four-carat pink diamond ring set in a twenty-four-carat gold band. He took Val's left hand, and slowly took off the forty-carat diamond wedding ring Victor had given her, then placed the sparkling pink ring on her finger.

"This is the ring I had in my pocket to give to you thirty some years ago before you went tumbling down the steps in your dorm at Howard and miscarried our baby. I have always kept it with me, praying one day that a miracle would bring us back together, and I could finally put it on your finger. This is just temporary. I may not have twenty-one billion dollars in the bank, but I have more than enough to compete with the ice I just removed from your finger."

Val put the wedding ring from Victor on the nightstand.

"You don't need to compete with anything or anyone, sweetheart." Holding up her hand, and smiling at the beautiful emerald cut bauble, Val said, "I love this ring. It is unbelievable that you hung on to it for over three decades. I don't ever intend to take it off."

The reunited lovers' bodies became one for the second time that night. They made love, blocking out the long, hard, and sad day they endured as if no one else in the world existed.

As Valerie and Royale reignited their flame, another budding relationship was in motion at the American Hotel in Sag Harbor. The hotel, an East End fixture was dated back to 1846. It provided a proud home for Sag Harbor's incredible group of residents, local and international, poor, and wealthy, struggling, famous, and unsavory clients as in Sincere Davidson, but also accomplished and powerful, published and unpublished, beautiful, and ordinary.

Sincere and his cousins had been coming to Sag Harbor since Royale signed his first baseball contract and purchased the old church and parsonage as a place to spend their summers. Sincere knew how much Royale and nosey celebrity snitch loved the American Hotel, so he went there knowing his cousin had to show up at some point. He needed to get some precious cargo out of Royale's Bugatti, even if he had to exterminate him.

When he walked in, Sincere noticed Turquoise sitting at a secluded table, listening to the piano player, Lee Glantz, singing the old Frank Sinatra hit, "That's Life." Looking incredibly beautiful with her cinnamon-colored skin and long reddish-brown locs hung to her waist. She was as beautiful as Rolondo had described. She was a woman he had wanted to meet for the last two years. Plus, she could be very useful to him.

Sliding into the empty chair at Turquoise's table, Sincere sang along with the crooner, slightly changing the lyrics.

"That's life, that's what all the people say, Rome and Royale are riding, high in April, shut down in May, but by killing them, I'm going to change that tune, when I'm back on top by June."

"Who are you?" Turquoise asked in a frightened whisper as she gulped her Apple Martini down.

"Allow me to introduce myself, gorgeous. I already know that you are Turquoise Hobson. My name is Sincere. I am the younger, and much better looking brother of the late Victor Dumas. I am also the late Rolondo Jemison's cousin, who I understand you knew as Royale Jones."

Before Turquoise could utter one word, the waiter approached them.

"Can I get you something to drink and a menu, sir?"

"Yes, please do. I'll have a double shot of Jack Daniels straight up, and you can bring the beautiful lady another glass of whatever she is drinking," answered Sincere.

"How do you know who I am?" asked Turquoise.

"I've had my eye on you ever since one of my business associate's nephew, the rapper DOD, spotted you at the Four Seasons Hotel two years ago having brunch with Rome Nyland and Valerie Rollins. I am the person who reminded Rolondo that he bought our factory from you, then persuaded him to pump you for information on Rome and Valerie. It did not take you but a Chicago minute to fall into Rolondo's trap. But once you crossed my cousin by testifying against him in court for your boyfriend, Rome, it was his idea to have the guys kidnap and drug you to put your fine ass on the hoestroll. That was a bad idea to fuck with Rolondo, baby. A bad idea. Now I have hit a stroke of luck running into you in this fine establishment tonight. Listening to reports from Rolondo and Yohance, I hear your sex game is mad tight. I could use a bonafide bitch like you in my stable. But you had better not try any tricks with me because I make Rolondo look like a rookie at bat for the first time."

The waiter came back at the table with their drinks.

Unnerved by this man's words, Turquoise took another quick sip of her drink. She had often heard Yohance talking on the telephone to a Sincere after the Bugatti Blades kidnapped her. Although she was unnerved, she had heard enough of Yohance's one-sided conversations with him to know he could kill her if she tried to get up and leave. It was safer to engage him in a conversation then make a mad dash for her room.

"Is Yohance still in prison?"

"You liked that junior flip dick, my pretty, didn't you? Yes, he's still in jail."

She refused to answer Sincere's sarcastic question. "What do you want from me? Turquoise asked him. "I plan to return to Los Angeles tomorrow. There is nothing here for me on the east coast. Rome is heavily into his new woman, Amethyst. He doesn't want me anymore."

Slowly sipping his bourbon, Sincere told her, "Amethyst cannot hold a candle to you. I know her. She has always been weak and afraid. I want you to get Rome back. I even want you to mend your problems with Valerie and get close to her. Look, I know you made a killing on selling that Bridgehampton compound to my dear departed brother. But I also know that you are a businesswoman. There can be a whole lot more millions in store for you if you work with me. And, on the real tip, as I said, I can use a woman with your intelligence and bedroom skills. Look how easy it was for you to cheat on Rome with my cousin. You are not a one man's woman, baby. We can bring Rome and Valerie down together, and get rid of the real Royale Jones while taking all of his money at the same time."

"I thought he was Rolondo earlier today and fainted. They look just alike."

"Their mothers were identical twins who married their fathers who were also identical twins."

"I'm curious," said Turquoise. "Valerie and this Royale seemed rather chummy today. How did that happen? He said something about them being in love when they were in college."

"Yes, that is true. Those two are hopeless. They are the original star-crossed lovers who have been soulmates since she was at Howard University, and he played on the University of Michigan's baseball team. I have been trying to get rid of her since she was nineteen-years-old to no avail. Rolondo thought he had killed Royale and took over his identity. But our dear cousin regained his memory after having amnesia for five years. I want both his and Victor's fortunes. It is finally time for his and Val's time on earth to come to an end! Royale has around one hundred million dollars in silver, gold bars, and coins hidden somewhere in Claude's church in a concrete bunker, which is not far from here. Rolondo tried to kill him nine years ago to find the location where his fortune is hidden. Claude and I have been looking through there for years and still cannot find a trace of that bounty. As I said, I need you to get back with Rome and close to Valerie. I'm positive Royale will tell Valerie about his silver and gold to compete with the money that Victor left her. He is a typical retired athlete. Those types of guys are always competitive. Part of that money should be mine. Victor built up his pharmaceutical and electronics company with the money that our father left him. As soon as we find out where that coin fortune is, and force Val and Vance to give up half of their money, they are history. I will get my hands on both of my brother and my cousin's cash. This little extermination could make you a member of the billionaire's club, Miss Real Estate Tycoon! Do we have a deal?"

Although every word that came out of that man's mouth terrified her, something within Turquoise made her think dealing with him would finally give her a satisfaction she looked for. Just thinking about all that money, and finally getting Valerie out of her life for good, was too tempting of an opportunity to turn down. She raised her glass to him.

"We have a deal!"

The waiter approached their table again, telling Sincere and Turquoise it was the last call.

"Give us a bottle of Cristal. This beautiful lady and I have a lot to celebrate!" Sincere said.

Gazing intensely into Turquoise's beautiful eyes, Sincere told her, "Baby, rolling with me is going to take you to a new level. I will make you forget you ever knew Rome, Rolondo, or Yohance. Welcome to the world of Sincere!"

"It sounds like the perfect blueprint for success to me!"

This new conniving duo were so caught up in their sinister plot, they never noticed Jamal from Vance's polo team, sitting at the bar, hanging onto their every word.

CHAPTER EIGHT

Valerie and Royale
Sunday Morning
Bugatti Blues

THE RINGING of Royale's phone combined with chimes coming from Valerie's intercom awakened the happy couple at the same time.

Royale looked at the digital clock on the cable box for Valerie's television.

"This can't be good. Who could be trying to contact both of us at six o'clock in the morning?"

"It's my kitchen staff letting me know breakfast is ready. I get up at six on the weekends and five thirty during the week," explained Val.

He nodded and picked up his phone.

A female voice was on the other end.

"Good morning. Is this Royale Jones?"

"Yes. This is Royale. Who am I speaking to?"

"My name is Johnyce Parks. I am the Assistant Pastor at the

Holy Temple of Mary Magdalene. Pastor Claude gave me your number. I know we are unable to hold a service at the church this morning, but I left some especially important belongings there and need to retrieve them right away."

"When did you speak to Claude? Is he still being held by the FBI?"

"He called me a little while ago. Yes, he is still being retained until his arraignment tomorrow."

"I'm sorry to have to tell you this, Reverend Parks, but services are going to be suspended at the church until further notice. For the time being, the police still have everything taped off because it is a crime scene, so no one is allowed in. Once the authorities clear everything, I will meet with you and see if we can come to some sort of understanding."

"But Mr. Jones, the funds to pay the staff are in the church's safe and I have quite a bit of my Sunday wardrobe there too. Can't you just let me in long enough to get those items," Pastor Johnyce pleaded.

Not wanting to offend a woman of the cloth, Royale told her, "I understand. All right. I can agree to letting you in to get your belongings from the church's office. Is ten o'clock this morning good?"

"Yes, ten o'clock is fine."

"Okay. I will see you then. Goodbye."

"God bless you."

Val dashed into the bathroom to wash up and get herself together. Coming back into the room, she sat down on the bed next to Royale.

"Is everything okay, darling?"

"Yes. That was Claude's assistant pastor. She wanted to get into the church to prepare for services today. I told her the church is closed for now, but I will meet her at ten to pick up some belongings she has there. Mind if I use your shower? I guess I should head back to the American Hotel before anyone discovers I spent the night here."

Val threw her arms around Royale's neck.

"I already laid out fresh towels, a toothbrush, and toothpaste for you in Victor's bathroom. The last time I checked the only name on the deed to this house is mine, so it is no one's business that you spent the night here. In fact, I would love it if you moved in here with me. There is no need for you to stay at a hotel. In all these years, we have never lived together. When we were young, we were either driving or flying back and forth between Washington D.C. and Ann Arbor, Michigan to see each other. I want to wake up next to you every morning."

"Baby, I have been waiting to hear those words come out of your mouth since I was twenty years old. We can get my stuff as soon as I take a shower. We can eat breakfast at the hotel." He proceeded to plant kisses all over Valerie's naked body.

CHAPTER NINE

Rome and Amethyst
Bullets For Brunch

A COUPLE OF HOURS LATER, Rome and Amethyst were heading back to the compound after their morning run. Amethyst stopped short when she saw Royale's car parked in front of the garage where Val kept her extensive car collection.

"Look at this gorgeous Bugatti. It had to cost at least a million dollars. Is it Valerie's?"

"No," answered Rome. "It belongs to Royale."

"Royale? I wonder why he left the car here last night."

With a small laugh, Rome told her, "Although I am not a betting man, I would put money on Royale still being in his car. I will go ahead and assume that Val broke down and finally gave the poor guy some."

Amethyst could not believe what she was hearing.

"They haven't had sex again yet? I had no idea that Royale had enough money to own a million –dollar car. Playing with the Los Angeles Wildcats must have paid well!"

"To answer both of your questions, no. Val wanted to wait to resume their physical relationship out of respect for Victor, and, yes, apparently Royale can afford a nice toy like this car."

"From the great Black billionaire, Victor Dumas, to a very wealthy retired baseball player," exclaimed Amethyst. "How does a woman as old as Valerie, who doesn't exactly have an hour-glass figure, keep attracting that caliber of men? I mean, how does she even meet them?"

"She met Victor through me. He hired me to find his wife, Andrea, who was missing. Val discovered that Andrea was dead, and her friend, Jermonna Bradley, was also shot at the same club in Las Vegas, which is ironically owned by Royale. The same day that I introduced Victor to Valerie, he told me that he had been watching her on television for years as well as reading her columns, and that she was a woman he had always wanted to meet. As for Val's relationship with Royale, they were college sweethearts, so there is a lot of history between them. I cannot believe you are talking about Val like this, Amethyst. You are starting to remind me of Turquoise, and that is not a good thing, sweetheart! She is extremely jealous of Val. Please don't go there with me."

Before Amethyst could respond to Rome, a glowing Val and Royale walked toward the car with their arms wrapped around each other.

"Good morning, guys," Val said.

"I don't know how good of a morning it is, but it looks like you two had a great night," Rome said as he slapped Royale five. He noticed his partner was a bit dressed up in a lovely gold knit dress by B. Michael.

"Where are you headed to?" Rome asked.

"To meet with a woman who says she is the assistant pastor of Claude's church, and then to the

American Hotel for brunch. I am glad you are out here

though, Rome. Both Sincere and Claude keep talking about this car. I need to check something out."

Royale popped his trunk open and then removed the floor of the trunk. There was a hidden compartment beneath it. He opened it with another key and pulled out a large Louis Vuitton suitcase.

"Some things never change," said Royale. "I see these fools are still up to their old tricks." Using another key, he slowly opened the suitcase. Sifting through its contents, the now astounded group saw it was filled with a gun, bullets, cocaine, ecstasy, marijuana, heroin, pain killers, and prescription strength cough syrup.

Shaking his head, Royale asked, "What could they have been using the cough syrup for?"

"It's often used to make a concoction called Purple Drank," answered Amethyst.

She had gulped down more than enough of it when she was getting high to know exactly what the cough syrup was for.

Royale opened his old Louis Vuitton portfolio and pulled out a wad of one hundred dollar bills.

"It looks like there is about fifty thousand dollars in cash in here."

"Should I call the police?" asked Valerie.

"No, baby," answered Royale. "I'm calling Sincere and giving all of this contraband back to him. If we call the cops it will give him one more reason to try to kill us. Plus, they could even hold me as a suspect. Yesterday was the first time I've been in this car since the night Rolondo thought he killed me ten years ago."

"He's right, Val. All of this makes him look like a prime suspect. If I hadn't been with him yesterday, when he took the car back from Claude, I would even be suspicious," said Rome. "Dial him up, Royale."

Royale spoke into his phone. "Call Sincere." He picked up on the first ring.

"What do you want, cousin?"

"I found something that I am sure belongs to you under the trunk of my car. I am at Valerie's. Come get it right now."

"Wise decision, cousin. Wise decision. What you do not know is I have some guys who have been very close to your present location all night long with fingers just itching to pull the triggers on their guns and take my belongings from you. I will instruct them to pull right up and claim everything. Do not try anything slick. I am not quite ready to kill your lame ass yet. I am dreaming of it raining gold and silver before I rid the world of you finally. Bye for now."

Rome dialed Dwayne on the house phone.

"Yes, boss?"

"Grab Kahari and two other guys and gear up. I need you at the front gate now."

"You got it," said Dwayne.

Rome then told Val, "You and Amethyst go back inside and gather up everyone and go to the safe room. I'll get you as soon as this hand off is over."

"All right. Be careful you two."

The ladies headed inside as Dwayne and his crew, carrying guns, and wearing bulletproof vests, ran past them.

"Are you ready, Royale?" asked Rome.

"Yes, let's do this."

Dwayne slowly opened the gate.

A black Cadillac Escalade with dark tinted windows drove up the driveway and came to a stop.

Flanking Royale with their guns drawn, Rome and the guys slowly walked towards the car. The door on the passenger side slowly opened, and a teenager got out. Royale handed him the suitcase, he hopped back into the car, and the car sped off.

"Thank you, Rome," said Royale.

"No problem. I totally agreed with you that it was better to give Valerian that stuff back. I have learned how his mind works over the years. Revenge runs through his veins instead of blood. He is a stone-cold gangster. It is amazing, though, that he has never done any time for the crimes that he has committed over so many years."

"That's because he has innocent kids like that young man we just encountered as the front men for his dirty deeds to do the time for him. My cousin is going to get caught one day though. Sincere always stayed below the radar, living mainly in Switzerland, just slithering in and out of the United States whenever it was necessary. But since Victor found out about his existence, Sincere has become more visible. With visibility comes vulnerability. He is going to slip up real soon," said Royale.

"I'll be glad when something or other puts his ass in jail. I am tired of this daily drama," said Rome.

Changing the subject, he asked Royale, "Do you know this minister you and Val are meeting at the church?"

"No, I've never met her. Why?"

"It could be another trap. I am going to send Dwayne with you and Val. Meanwhile, I'll also call the Sag Harbor police and ask them if a couple of officers can meet you there too. You were right on target with your hunch that the authorities could have arrested you for those drugs, cash, and guns in your car, but you may need some back-up when you get to the church. I am going to go tell Val it's okay for everyone to leave the safe room now."

"Okay. By the way, I proposed to Val last night."

"Really, what did she say?" asked Rome.

"She said yes. We are officially engaged!"

Shaking Royale's hand, Rome told him, "Congratulations." He then headed inside to get Valerie.

65

CHAPTER TEN

Pastor Johnyce
Sins of The Saints

THE THREAT of Royale almost getting involved in Valerian's illegal doings earlier that morning had slowed Val and Royale's progress down. After making sure Valencia and her nanny were safe and well-guarded, the newly betrothed twosome drove straight to the church instead of stopping at the hotel. Dwayne trailed closely behind them.

A stunning young woman, who looked to be in her late twenties, stood in front of the Holy Temple of Mary Magdalene. She was wearing a bright purple mini-dress that left little to the imagination with matching six-inch stiletto heels. Flinging her waist long braids, she smiled at Royale, Dwayne, and Val as they approached her.

Shaking Royale's hand, she said, "Good morning, Mr. Jones. I am Reverend Johnyce Parks, but please call me Pastor Johnyce. Thank you for meeting me here."

"This is my fiancé, Valerie Rollins," said Royale. With her

reporter's instinct kicking in, Val looked closely at Pastor Johnyce. It was obvious the girl was much more of a pimp's pawn than a preacher. There was no way she was allowing Royale to let her enter his property. She could smell the danger waiting to happen inside if he did. Little did she know, it didn't matter whether they were inside or outside, danger and heartbreak were ahead.

"It is nice to meet you," said Valerie. "I have to say you look more like a bronze beauty queen than a minister. You ladies have come a long way from wearing a white collar and a boring black dress or suit."

"I am Pastor Claude's protégé," said Johnyce. "He feels that our young parishioners can relate much better to my ministering if my wardrobe is trendy."

Val smiled.

"I can understand that. This is our security guard, Dwayne. Would you mind showing him your identification before we enter the building. It would also be nice if you have a card with your name and position with the church on it."

Holding up a small purple alligator clutch, Johnyce said, "I only brought this tiny bag with me that isn't big enough to hold my wallet. I left all of that stuff at home."

As they stood there, a squad car pulled up and two officers got out.

"Is there a problem out here, pastor?" asked one of them.

Royale recognized him as Officer Weaver, who had not inspected the parsonage the day before.

"There really isn't a problem, Officer Weaver. However, my fiancé just wants to make sure the lovely pastor is who she says she is before I let her into my property to reclaim whatever belongings she has in there. You and I met yesterday. I am Pastor Claude's cousin, Royale Jones."

Johnyce didn't like what was happening. She didn't really

leave her belongings in the church's office. Aside from ministering to the sick and homeless, her position at the church was to operate Claude's call girl ring from out of there. Not expecting this man, Royale, to show up with a woman, she had dressed to seduce him. Her original plan was unraveling before her eyes. She decided to shift gears and make a cat move. She would make friends with his woman.

Before she could utter one word, shots rang out as a car sped by. Dwayne crumpled to the ground.

"Dwayne!" Valerie screamed, dropping down to her knees beside him.

The officers drew their guns as Val quickly dialed 9-1-1.

"My security guard, Dwayne Douglas, has just been shot. We are in front of the Holy Temple of Mary Magdalene in Sag Harbor. Please get here as fast as you can."

She took a wad of tissues out of her purse, and applied them to Dwayne's head as blood flowed from it.

Royale got on his knees next to Val, pulling her close to him. It was obvious one of the shots fired were aimed directly for the middle of Dwayne's head. He was gone. This was no random shooting.

Being shot at was not supposed to be on her agenda this morning, so Pastor Johnyce decided to flee the scene. She would figure how to get into the church later.

"Mr. Jones, I am going to leave. I do not feel comfortable staying here with this poor man dying in front of me. We can talk about me retrieving my things another day."

The ambulance came screeching to a halt and the paramedics raced to Dwayne's body.

"You are not going anywhere until you tell me who sent you to set me up! Was it my cousin, Sincere? Who told you to lure us into this trap?" Royale yelled at her.

"No one told me anything about gunfire. I was just

supposed to get you to tell me where you have the gold and silver buried. I don't know why we were shot at! I am not into gun violence. I am an ordained minister as well as a preacher's kid. I would not try to get anybody killed!"

Valerie stood up to let the paramedics do their job. In her heart of hearts, she knew her friend was no longer with them in the flesh. Her next call was to Rome.

"You have a lot of explaining to do. Why did I have to hear it from Royale that you two are engaged. Why didn't you tell me?" Rome asked.

Unable to withhold her tears, Val said, "I can't talk about that now, Rome. Dwayne got shot in a drive-by in front of Claude's church. He's dead."

Without hesitation, Rome said, "We're on the way there now."

"The medical examiner is getting ready to take Dwayne's body to the morgue. Why don't you pick up Vance and Kwami and meet us at the American Hotel? Royale and I still have to go over there so he can check out and pick up his belongings."

"Where is he going?"

"He's moving in with me," said Val. "This is something that we have waited a long time for to happen. Life is getting shorter by the minute."

"I hear you. Okay, we will head to the hotel. Stay in Royale's room until we arrive."

"You got it."

As the paramedics rolled Dwayne's body to the van, Val told them, "I am going to take his wallet and phone with me. Let me just hand you his identification. Where are you taking him?"

"To the morgue at Stony Brook Southampton Hospital, ma'am," said one of the EMT workers. "You should be able to identify his body there after they formally pronounce Mr. Douglas dead."

His last five words were unbelievable to Valerie.

"I can't believe he just used the words, *formally pronounce Mr. Douglas dead,*" she said to Royale, with tears still pouring down her face. "Dwayne has been by my side since I first started dating Victor."

Royale held her tightly. "I am so sorry, baby. I feel like I have blood on my hands, and this is all my fault. I should not have brought you with me this morning."

"Then you might be dead, and I really couldn't have handled that."

More uniformed policemen were putting crime scene tape around the lawn in front of the church as an inquisitive crowd gathered.

"Mr. Jones, you and the lady are free to go. Just one question, do you have any idea who may have been trying to kill you or your security guard?" asked Officer Weaver.

"Yes. Without a doubt, my cousins, Valerian Davidson and Claude Hoskins. You witnessed Claude trying to shoot me yesterday."

"That is correct. But Pastor Claude is still in custody in New York City. I understand he will not be arraigned until tomorrow. I know that Mr. Davidson has been released, but he has no priors and no connection to any of the victims or crimes that were committed, so I am ruling both out as suspects of this murder that occurred here today."

"Since you just told us that we can leave right now, that's what my fiancé and I will do. You still have my information that I gave to you yesterday. Call me if you hear anything."

Handing her card to Officer Weaver, Val told him, "Please call me as soon as the medical examiner is ready for someone to identify my friend's body and release his remains."

"Will do. My condolences."

Val turned her attention to Pastor Johnyce.

"I don't know or care who you are. All I know is my friend is dead because you asked Royale to meet you here. Whether you want to or not, you are coming with us so my partner, Rome, and I can question you. Get in the car with us now."

"But my car is here."

"We will bring you back here to get it as soon as we finish," said Royale. He held the door open for her to squeeze into the tiny back seat.

As soon as they got into the car, Val told Royale, "That cop Weaver is dirty. He didn't look the least bit surprised when he heard the shots."

"You are so right. I have a question to ask you. Baby, was Dwayne already working for Victor when you two got together?"

"Yes, he worked for him for many years on the horse farm in Kentucky. Why do you ask?"

"I thought he looked familiar. I've seen him somewhere before I ran into you guys the other year."

"Are you sure?"

"Just like Sincere possibly being Vance's dad, I am almost positive. I remember a guy named Dwayne hanging around when we were teenagers who moved to Illinois from Milwaukee."

As they pulled up in front of the hotel, visibly shivering and still teary eyed after being so close to flying bullets, Val said, "I am so weary of all of these near death experiences that have occurred since I met Victor. And it all seems to go back to Andrea. If I had not seen her body lying on the floor in that back room of what I now know was your social club in Las Vegas, I would swear she is still alive, sending out evil vibes to surround us. Let's go retrieve your belongings from the hotel.

This is starting to be a little too much of six degrees of separation for me."

Royale tenderly caressed Valerie's cheek. "I'm back in your world now, sweetheart. No one is ever going to hurt you. I will protect you with my life."

CHAPTER ELEVEN

A Collision of Cousins
Sunday Morning

Rome, Vance, Kwami, and Kahari entered the hotel's lobby simultaneously as Valerian and Turquoise sat down to have brunch in the restaurant. Neither party saw the other one as they narrowly missed crossing paths.

Rome called Val.

"We're downstairs. Come on down."

"All right. Listen, Royale and I never got a chance to have dinner last night. I am starving. Can we eat here before we go home? We also have the minister that we went to meet with us. She may have orchestrated Dwayne's murder."

"No, I didn't!" yelled Johnyce in the background.

Overhearing Johnyce, Rome told Valerie, "She seems to be a high-spirited one. That is fine with me. I have not eaten today either. I'll get a table for seven."

Before he told the hostess how many people were in his party, Rome heard Valerian's voice.

"Well, well, well, the gang is still here. It is so nice to see you this morning, son."

Ignoring Valerian, Vance told the hostess whom he was familiar with in a biblical sense, "I need a table for seven, Amy."

"I'll get that set up in the back for you right away, Mr. Dumas. Feel free to have a drink in the lobby while we get it ready."

"Thank you, baby."

As they sat down on a couch, Turquoise came out of the bathroom.

Startled by her ex-fiancé's presence, she exclaimed, "Rome! I did not expect to see you here this morning."

"I can say the same thing about you."

Valerian stood up from his table and made his way over to Turquoise. He put his arm possessively around her.

"The lady is with me. I am sure you know the old saying, *one man's ex is another man's treasure.*"

Rome glared at Turquoise and Valerian.

Getting off the elevator and surveying the situation, Val asked, "How did you two get together? I should talk about you for my 'Hot New Couple Alert' on my radio show tomorrow. This is too funny. Both of you are slumming."

"I see that when it comes to women, you still move in on everyone else's relationship, Sincere, which included Victor's with Andrea." Royale smirked.

"I am going to pretend like I didn't hear those words come out of your mouth, cousin," said Valerian.

Vance jumped up and hugged Val.

"What happened to Dwayne? He was like an uncle to me. He lived on the farm with us since I was

my daughter's age. Who would do this to him, Val?"

"I don't know, sweetie. But Rome and I are on it, so we will have an answer for you soon."

The awkward moment ended as the hostess told Vance that his table was ready.

"Before you sit down to eat, Sincere, I need to speak with you. Val's security guard was just shot and killed in front of the church. In fact, do you know this young lady, Pastor Johnyce? Since she is connected to Claude and the Tabernacle, it makes sense to me that you two would also be acquainted with one another," Royale said.

Devouring her body with his eyes, Sincere told him, "No, I have never seen this delectable beauty in my life, but I would not mind getting to know her. She has a face and body I would never forget. I do not have anything to do with Claude's church business nor the stable of women who work for him. And before you ask, I did not have a damn thing to do with Dwayne's death. He served no purpose in my life, so there is no reason for me to want him dead."

Feeling as if she was being visually raped, Johnyce told Royale, "He is telling the truth. Although I have heard Pastor Claude mention his cousin, Sincere, this is the first time I have ever met this gentleman."

Clasping Royale's hand, Val said, "Why don't we sit down and eat? Then we can sort out this horror story we just witnessed. I am grieving right now for Dwayne. I do not know what or who to believe because all you do is keep secrets and tell lies, Valerian."

"And I enjoy doing both," quipped Sincere.

As the group walked to their table, Turquoise stopped Rome.

"Can we please talk before you leave?"

"It's against my better judgement, but yes, we can talk. Enjoy your brunch."

"Smooth move, baby," whispered Sincere when Rome walked away. "Our little arrangement is going to work out simply fine. Let us sit back down. Our food is just arriving."

As they arrived at their table in the back, Vance also had eyes on Johnyce. He held out a chair for her.

"Please, sit next to me, pastor. I am in need of ministering. In fact, I am so sinful that I could use the work of an exorcist."

"I don't know if I can provide all of that for you, but it would be an honor to sit by you, Mr. Dumas. I'm a huge fan of yours."

Rome couldn't resist taking a crack at Vance's remark.

"Since when did you need a minister, Vance?" asked Rome. "When is the last time you went to church?"

"It was a long time ago. That's why I need Pastor Johnyce to lay her hands on me."

If she hadn't been so devastated over Dwayne, Val would have laughed at Vance and his corny rap. Her phone began blowing up with text messages.

While they were in Royale's room, she had texted her source Johnyce's information to see what he could find out about her. He came back with some good stuff. After asking the waitress for a glass of chardonnay, while she handed each of them menus, Valerie addressed the pastor.

"Okay, your name is really Johnyce Parks. So why didn't you want to show us your identification?"

"I really don't have it with me, Ms. Rollins."

"I understand that you're an Evangelists of the Flesh LLC does more than preach at the church. I have just been told there is an escort business that is sadly based there," Val said, continuing.

"Yes, that is true. I am not ashamed if it. That is why Pastor Claude named the place of worship after Saint Mary Magdalene. According to the scripture, she was a prostitute, who gave her life to God. When the disciples abandoned Jesus, at the hour of mortal death, Mary of Magdala was one of the women who stayed with him, even to the crucifixion. She was present at the tomb; the first person to whom Jesus appeared after his resurrection and the first to preach the *Good News* of that miracle. Yes, I am an Evangelist of the Flesh, and I see nothing ungodly about giving men pleasure. I can assure you, though, I had nothing to do with the murder of your friend. I look at my adult business as a ministry to men in need. I am a hoe, not a killer."

She spoke so passionately that Valerie believed her.

"You remind me a lot of my best friend, Jermonna Bradley."

"The actress? I don't look anything like her."

"No, you don't. But you have the same kind of will and could care less about what people think of you. I like strong women like you two ladies," said Valerie.

"Pastor, for all of our sakes, I hope you are not as whacked out as Jermonna. I've been begging Val to leave that little nut job alone since I met her, "Rome said.

Val interjected. "Rome, we are not having this meeting with Pastor Johnyce for you to put down Jermonna."

"You're the one who brought her up," he said, laughing.

"Getting back to you, Johnyce, I am never one to knock anyone's hustle. But why did Claude tell you to get Royale over to the church this morning since that so-called pastor is nothing but a closet pimp?" asked Rome.

"Like Mary stood by Jesus, I will always be devoted to Pastor Claude. I was a teenage runaway, turning tricks in Times Square for crack when I met him. He took me under his wing, got me cleaned up, and sent me to seminary school. I consider him to be more of a Savior to me than my pimp. But if you must know, the reason for me calling Mr. Jones, is that Pastor Claude wanted me to find out where he has some silver and gold hidden. He thought I could charm him into telling me."

Val looked at Royale.

"Honey, what is with all of this gold and silver talk? Your cousin over there said he wanted it to be raining gold and silver last night."

"I'll discuss it with you and Rome tonight," Royale said.

"Okay, baby. Why don't you guys order some drinks and look at these menus?"

As the guys ordered drinks, Vance sparked a conversation with Johnyce.

"Do you drink, gorgeous one?"

"Yes, I do."

He summoned the waiter.

"Three bottles of Louis Roederer for the table along with two pitchers of orange juice. I am mourning the loss of my uncle but celebrating the introduction to whom I hope will become a very good friend. So, we will make a toast to Dwayne's memory and what the future may bring!"

"I'll be right back with everything, Mr. Dumas."

Rome looked at the menu. "They are calling this *the out of lockdown menu!* That's a good gimmick.," Rome commented.

"Now that the vaccine is being distributed to everyone, there is light at the end of the tunnel for this pandemic," commented Kwami.

Two bus boys came back with the champagne, orange juice, and glasses for everyone.

"Is everyone ready to order?" asked the waiter.

"Yes," answered Val. "I'll have the smoked rainbow trout garni to start and the sirloin steak maître d'hôtel medium. Thank you. How about you, pastor?"

"I'll try the lobster bacon, lettuce and tomato sandwich. I

have never heard of lobster being used in a BLT. It sounds delicious."

"I'm sure it's nowhere near as delicious as you probably taste, baby," said Vance. "You can also bring me the steak and the house salad to start."

"I'll have what Val ordered," said Royale.

"You can make that three of us," said Rome.

"I'll just have a chicken salad sandwich," said Kwami. "I don't have much of an appetite thinking about Dwayne being gone. I started working part-time at Dumas Farms when I was just fifteen. He was like my uncle too."

"With everything that has been popping off this weekend, I haven't had a chance to eat either. I'll go with the steak too, and your Soup de Jour to start," said Kahari.

Vance held up his glass. "To Dwayne and sweet Johnyce!"

CHAPTER TWELVE

Aurora
Silver Ridge Healthcare Center
Las Vegas

As the group in Sag Harbor mourned Dwayne's death, a woman with skin the color of smooth, dark brown velvet and curly gray hair that cascaded down to her waist, was feeling satisfied in Las Vegas.

Her plan to kill the Judas like bastard had gone off without a hitch. Although she had married one man for his money, and another for the great sex combined with drugs he happily supplied to her, Aurora and Dwayne had been in love since they were teenagers. The first internationally known full-figured supermodel, she loved to party! So did Sincere. He was the ultimate Svengali, who taught her how to manipulate her way through life.

Ten years ago, that son of a bitch shot her several times over a drug deal gone wrong.

Believing she was dead, he got out of Las Vegas faster than

the speeding bullets that riddled her head and body. Dwayne, who was also there, stayed hidden beneath a trap door where another woman, Premise, was shot and killed. While the detectives canvassed the Wildcats Social Club outside, he snuck back into the room where Aurora laid on the floor and noticed she was still breathing under the sheet placed over her.

He quickly went back down into the secret room, picked up Premise's body, then took her upstairs, and put her under the sheet. He then picked up Aurora and took her out a secret exit that led to a hidden garage. From there, Dwayne called a doctor that had removed bullets from victims before. The doctor told him to take Aurora to the back entrance of the Silver Ridge Healthcare Center. Aurora's husband, whom she had always hated, never asked for a viewing of her body, so Premise was cremated in her place. To the world, she was dead. However, Aurora was very much alive and lived in the facility all these years.

It was miraculous she survived the shooting because it left bullets in her head, shoulder, back, and leg. For the past eight years, she had undergone physical, speech, and occupational therapy.

Silver Ridge also had an excellent wound care and skin management program. Like Humpty Dumpty, they slowly put her back together again.

Although her husband and lover thought she died broke, she had always kept a vault size safe deposit box at the Bank of Nevada that had three million dollars in cash, along with around two million dollars' worth of jewelry. Her husband had always been a generous man. She knew she could trust Dwayne, so she signed papers allowing him access to the box and that was how she paid for the treatment over the years. Now that she could walk and talk again, she was discharged.

She asked Dwayne to kill her old lover, which he had many opportunities to do.

Instead, he told her, "Aurora, we are too old for this gang activity. Just go to Sincere when you get out of Silver Ridge and come to some sort of understanding. I cannot kill him. I have a nice life. I won't risk getting locked up, even for you."

Then, to make matters worse, Dwayne went on to say he planned to tell Sincere and Claude, as well as Vance and Valerie, she was still alive. Aurora couldn't allow Dwayne to do that. The suggestion left her so enraged that she knew she had to kill him.

Dwayne had no idea she stayed connected with some young Bugatti Blades in Las Vegas. For ten thousand dollars, two round trip plane tickets to New York, and a rental car, Dwayne had drawn his last breath today.

The first thing she was going to do when she was discharged was check into a suite at Caesars Palace, then head to the bar and party harder than an alcoholic on a never ending binge. She hadn't had a sip of liquor in a decade. From there, she would take care of lover boy, her son, and the woman masquerading as her late husband's widow herself.

She had always believed in self- preservation, as well as revenge being such a sweet thing! Aurora Darden was about to be back on top. She was ready for the new chapter in her life to begin. The time had come for this this deadly diva to make one last call to have one last call.

CHAPTER THIRTEEN

The American Hotel
Sag Harbor, New York

"Do any of you want dessert?" asked the waiter, as Valerie and the crew's brunch winded down.

"I'll just have another glass of chardonnay for the road," said Val. "Would you like some dessert, Johnyce?"

"Coffee is fine."

Vance leaned into her, asking, "Why don't you let me take you somewhere else for dessert? Mary J. Blige is having a tasting for her new Sun Goddess wine collection from six to eight at the Brooklyn Chop House in the city. If we leave now, we can get there on time."

"I love Mary J. Blige. I would love to join you, but my car is still over at the church."

"No problem, gorgeous. We can pick it up tonight when we get back."

"All right."

"I thought you rode over here with Rome and Kahari, Vance?" asked Val.

"No, I promised some people I would meet them at the wine tasting, so Kwami and I came in my Limo," he continued. "Val, Rome, Royale, Kahari, I will see you in a few days. Kwami and I are going to Terrell, Texas tomorrow to look at a couple of Arabian horses that I want to buy."

"I'll call you later. I would feel better if I sent a couple of extra security guys to Texas with you," said Rome.

"That's fine with me," he told Rome.

"Johnyce, are you ready?"

Standing up, she said, "Yes, I am. Thank you, Valerie, for brunch. I am so sorry about your friend. Mr. Jones has my number if you need me for anything else."

"We will definitely be in touch with you tomorrow. Please call me if you hear anything pertaining to Dwayne's murder," answered Val, handing her a card.

Once Vance and Johnyce were out of earshot, Val told Rome and Royale, "I actually like her. But can Vance go after any women who aren't strippers or call girls? First, he was married to Roshonda. She may be a gorgeous reality starlet, but her career began as an escort working for my friend Rebecca. Now he has a live-in strip club going on at his house, and now this girl tells us, she's a 'hoe not a killer.' Talk about having a type!"

"Baby, like many men, Vance is attracted to women who reminds them of their mothers. Andrea may have been a world renowned model, but she was a stone cold whore. He may not have liked her, but it is obvious to me he loved her very much," said Royale.

Sipping her wine, Val said, "Well, I wish he could find a woman that isn't just looking to make fast money, like an actress, singer, model. What is wrong with a professional woman? Maybe even a Solange Knowles type. I have always told people if I had a daughter, I would like her to be like Solange. She does not hide in her sister's, Beyonce, shadow. She has her own career and moves to the beat of her own drum. For example, she recently celebrated the two-year anniversary of her 2019 project, "When I Get Home," and admitted to the media that she was 'fighting for her life' while recording the album. She said she was 'in and out of hospitals. . . with depleting health and broken spirits asking God to send her a sign she would not only survive but that if he let her make it out alive, she would step into the light, whatever that meant. That is the kind of young woman that Vance needs. I wish I knew her and could introduce the two of them!"

"Will there be anything else?" asked the waiter.

"No, thank you. I'll take the check," said Val.

As the waiter handed the check to her, Royale took it, placed his credit card in it, and handed it back to the waiter.

"You are about to be my wife, and from now on, in our household, I will be paying for things."

"That is not necessary but thank you, kind sir. Your generosity deserves a kiss."

As Val kissed Royale, Turquoise sat down in the seat Vance had vacated next to Rome.

"Are you ready to talk, Rome?"

"Did I hear someone ask you to join us, Turquoise?" asked Valerie. "This stalking act you've got going on is making you look more desperate than usual."

"It's okay, Val. I want to hear what she has to say," said Rome.

"All right. In that case, Royale and I will see you back at the house where I believe you left Amethyst."

Val reached into her Naomi Osaka for Louis Vuitton handbag and handed Dwayne's phone and wallet to Rome.

"I almost forgot. Here is Dwayne's wallet and phone. You need to unlock it so we can see if anything unusual was going on with him. I am still having a hard time digesting that one minute Dwayne was standing next to me, and in a flash he was dead. Royale thinks that Dwayne may have been a guy they used to know when they were teenagers."

"Really?" asked Rome.

Royale signed the check and told Rome, "Yeah, I told Val I thought he looked familiar. Glancing at Turquoise, he told Rome, "Good luck, brother! I think you have been hanging around Vance too long. We will see you back at Valerie's house."

"Okay. When I get there, I'll follow up on your tip that Dwayne may have been connected to you guys in the past and look through his room. I don't think he had any next of kin, but I'll find out."

Royale and Val headed out.

Royale picked up his luggage from the concierge as they left the hotel, where they ran smack dab into Valerian. "Going somewhere, cousin?" Valerian asked.

"Where I am going is none of your business! Are you sure you don't know anything about Dwayne's murder? As I recall, he used to hang out around you and Claude when I was in college."

"I knew the fool from a distance. And once again, I did not have anything to do with what transpired this afternoon. I am heading out of town for a while, but neither of you had better get comfortable. You both owe me money, and I intend to get my hands on it one way or another. Good afternoon!"

Valerie was sick and tired of Valerian's never ending threats, so she decided to put an end to it.

"Valerian, prior to Victor's death, I realize that you turned down his offer to give you one billion dollars to stay away from our family, which includes Vance and Valencia. I have to talk it over with Vance, but I would like to double the money my late husband was willing to let you have from Dumas Electronics, and offer you two billion dollars to leave us alone. That's more than fair. Victor did start his company by selling the drug stores that your father owned. If Vance gives me the okay, I will have the money wired wherever you want it to go. Between the pandemic and your daily threats, I'm tired of living like this."

"I rightly deserve ten billion dollars, which is half of Dumas Electronics, but I will think about your offer. You can start with getting me a debit card in my name with a ten-million-dollar credit line by end of business day tomorrow. I will still be here at the hotel, at least until then."

"If I meet this demand, I want at least a five-day moratorium on all the madness. Do I have Sincere or Valerian Davidson put on the card?"

"Sincere Davidson is fine. I will give you my answer by Friday. And I am serious that I did not have Dwayne shot."

"You are one greedy piece of work, Sincere," said Royale. "Come on, Valerie, let's go."

As soon as they were outside, on the hotel's famous front porch, he asked Val, "Do you really want to give Sincere all that money, sweetheart? Just because he is Victor's brother does not mean he deserves that kind of bank. He didn't do anything to earn it."

As they got into the car, Val said, "I could care less how much money it will take to make him go away because I cannot spend another moment living like this. If Vance agrees to it, after I pay Valerian off, I also want to sell Dumas Electronics and live peacefully. I just want to enjoy life with you. Speaking of which, please tell me what is up with this silver and gold Valerian keeps talking about?"

"I have been collecting bars of gold and rare silver coins for years. It's worth around four-hundred- million dollars now. I also have around twenty-five million dollars in cash stashed. I should not have gotten involved, but remember I admitted to you that when I first retired from baseball, I used to finance some of their illegal activities. I also cleaned up their money from drug profits through my sports bar in Las Vegas. Rolondo was trying to steal my fortune when he thought he had killed me. He thought I had the cash stashed on my small yacht."

"Let me guess. Everything is at the church."

"You are right. The church was a stop on the underground railroad. There are two hidden trap doors beneath a pew and one under the altar that leads to hidden rooms. No one will ever find them. To top that off, the safes down there have combinations on them with your birthdate written backwards. Some of it is also hidden under a trap door in a safe built into a closet at my club in Las Vegas. I am trying to figure out a way to cash it all in as soon as possible. But I know that Sincere and Claude are having me closely watched. I just need to wait for the right time and hire an armored car and a lot of security guards. Both here and in Vegas."

"Good grief! Hearing all of this makes it even more important that I pay Valerian off. Maybe that will also make him leave you alone. Marriage is a partnership. I will do whatever I have to do to get that sociopath off our backs!"

"I know that we are partners, baby, but like I said when the check came for dinner, no matter how much bank you have, I am taking care of you. I like you referring to us as already being married. When do you want that to happen?"

"I'm ready right now. We have wasted far too much time. I have always wanted to get married in Las Vegas. We can do it next week."

Before Royale could comment, his phone rang.

"Royale Jones here."

"Good afternoon, Mr. Jones. This is Agent Smith Perry of the FBI. I just want you to know that Claude Hoskins will be arraigned in the morning in federal court in downtown Manhattan around eleven o'clock in case you would like to attend."

"No, I think I'll pass on being there. With all that has happened the last couple of days, I think it's best if my fiancé and I stay close to home this week and let matters cool down. Please call me after the arraignment and let me know what transpired."

"Will do. Goodbye."

"Claude is being arraigned in the morning in Manhattan. An FBI agent just asked me if I want to attend, but I think we need to stay put on your property for the rest of the week with back-to-back murders in two days."

"You are so right. I am going to call my personal banker at home tonight so that he can get Valerian the debit card first thing in the morning."

CHAPTER FOURTEEN

Valerie and Royale
A Home Is Where the Heart Is

THEY WERE FINALLY PULLING up to Valerie's estate. It had been another long, traumatic morning.

"I'm going to take a bath as soon as I get in the house to wash Dwayne's death off me, call my banker, and then write tomorrow's radio show. When Rome gets back, I'll help him look through Dwayne's belongings. Since it is Sunday, I am pretty sure that we won't hear from the coroner's office until tomorrow," said Val. "Jonelle serves Sunday dinner at six."

"You are one organized woman," Royale told Valerie. "That is precisely why I need your help with the Sag Harbor Scorpions. I also need to hire an assistant and rent some office space in Sag Harbor as well as in Manhattan."

As she got out of the car, Val said, "Let's go for a quick ride on one of the golf carts. I have something I want to show you."

They got into one of the four golf carts lining the gate, heading back to the main house.

Royalewas surprised it turned into a small road. "I didn't realize that you had all of this property back here, sweetheart," he said.

They stopped in front of a cul-de-sac of three ranch style homes that surrounded a small swimming pool.

"The house on the left is Rome's. The one in the middle belongs to Jonelle. But the one on the right is empty. Let's go inside. The door stays unlocked since no one lives here."

Royale was astounded again when they walked in.

"This living room is pretty big."

"Yes, it is great. There are three bedrooms and two and a half bathrooms. Welcome to the new office of the Sag Harbor Scorpions. Feel free to decorate it however you want to. If I were you, I would turn the living room into your reception area and your assistant's office. Then make the master bedroom your office because it has its own bathroom. Then make the other two rooms guest rooms in case any of your players have to stay overnight for some reason."

"Those are great ideas. This is a perfect location. Plus, you cannot beat the security here. But, baby, you must let me pay you some rent for this. I keep telling you that I am here to take care of you, not the other way around."

"Okay. How about one dollar a month? You do not have to pay rent. We are about to become husband and wife. As I said, this relationship is a partnership. I also have a huge office already set up in my apartment in New York City you can do business out of when you need to be in the city. I'm sure you will want to get new furniture though because it was Victor's office. The location will also work well because it is attached to a hotel and your players can stay there if they need to. I think I have your assistant problem solved too. Do you remember Cantrese, who used to be my assistant?"

"Yes. I do," answered Royale. "Wasn't she having an affair

with Vance while he was married to Violet and dating Roshonda?"

"That would be Cantrese," said Val. "She got tired of Vance's revolving harem of women. She met a nice guy, married him, then moved back to California. Unfortunately, that situation did not work out. She called me last week to tell me she would like to leave Los Angeles and come back to work for me. She can be our assistant."

"It all sounds like music to my ears. But, come on, love. You have got to let me pay Cantrese for working with both of us. Do you think two hundred thousand a year, plus insurance coverage is a good offer for her?"

Val smiled.

"That is a very generous offer. I will agree to you taking care of Cantrese's salary, and there is a studio guest house down near the stables that is unoccupied. She can live there. I'll call her and send the jet that Vance is not taking to Texas, to Los Angeles to pick her up. I am so happy that Cantrese is coming back. I miss her a lot. I am ready for that bath. Let's head to the main house."

Royale and Valerie walked out his new headquarters and ran into Amethyst, who was in the pool swimming. She got out, wearing a red bikini, leaving nothing to the imagination.

"Hey, you two! Where is Rome? He said he was going to meet you. I am deeply sorry about Dwayne, Valerie. He was a genuinely nice guy."

"Yes, he was," said Val. "His murder is just too much to take. From the moment my late husband introduced me to Dwayne, he treated me like royalty. Rome should be here soon. He had some additional business to take care of back at the hotel."

"What are you two up to out here?" asked Amethyst, giving Royale a thirsty look.

"We are turning this guest house into the main office for Royale's minor league baseball team," answered Val.

"I did not know you had a baseball team, Royale. You will have to tell me about it."

"I am in the beginning stages of putting it together. My beautiful fiancé here is helping me."

"We need to get back up to the house. I need to take care of that business regarding Valerian and get my radio show written and recorded for tomorrow. Unless you and Rome have other plans, Amethyst, I will see you up at the main house for cocktails at five, then dinner at six. I know it's harsh, but I need to keep up some sense of normalcy around here for Valencia's sake, as well as my own sanity. We are having pasta and a variety of seafood tonight. Sunday dinner around here is always nice," said Val.

"That sounds scrumptious," said Amethyst.

Okay, we'll see you later."

CHAPTER FIFTEEN

Vance and Johnyce
A Rapturous Ride

Vance's three and a half million dollars burgundy, bullet proof, stretched Rolls-Royce Phantom limousine was parked in front of the hotel. His driver, Cliff, jumped right out to open the back door for them, and then Kwami hopped in the front seat.

"I've never ridden in a vehicle this luxurious," said Johnyce. "I feel like I'm in the old Eddie Murphy Movie, 'Coming to America,' seeing all that opulence in Zamunda. I have loved that movie since I was a kid. I am really excited about the sequel, 'Coming 2 America.' I heard it is great!"

"This whip is a pretty special toy," said Vance. "I had it custom made. It is based on the Rolls-Royce Phantom Extended Wheelbase. However, this stretched version has over a meter of extras in between the axles. I love it almost as much as I love pussy and my horses."

"What kind of toys did you get for Christmas as a kid? I

barely got one doll. This is the first time that I have never even ridden in a Rolls-Royce."

"I only wanted horses for Christmas growing up. We will see how we get along, baby. If things work out the way I would like them to between us, I will wrap you up in a life filled with nothing but luxury."

Vance pulled up the carpet on the limo's floor and opened a built-in combination safe.

He counted out twenty-thousand dollars, then handed it to Johnyce.

"Do you always keep that kind of money in your car?"

"Why do you want to know that? You don't plan to rob me, or set me up like you might've did to my friend, do you?"

"Of course not. How many times do I have to tell you *people* that I did not set that man up? I am not that type of hoe!"

"You are going to have to tell me that you did not set up my 'people,' as you call them, as many times as I ask you."

Johnyce looked at Vance and rolled her eyes. "What is this money for anyway?"

Gently fingering her left breast, Vance told her," To start, this cash is for the blow job that you, are about to give me, and if it's as mind-blowing as I think it's going to be, it's also for the follow-up sex that is going to go down all the way into the city. You are the finest and sexiest thing I have encountered in a long time, baby. From the moment I laid my eyes on you, I knew I had to make you mine."

Slowly unzipping his pants, she asked him, "Aren't Ashro Chin and the Knox twins enough for you? Word on the hoe stroll is that the four of you have round the clock sex parties going on at your house, and that you paid them each one quarter of a million dollars to stay with you for the polo season."

"Look, I rarely drink and have never touched any illegal

substance. From the time I turned fourteen, sex has always been my drug. I am not going to deny that the throuple and I are having a lot of fun. However, there is something special about you that I have the urge to taste. I don't know what it is, but I intend to find out right now."

He reached into his pants and pulled out his penis. She engulfed it into her mouth.

"Vance, baby, I am going to make you feel so good, you are going to send those amateur strippers that you have ensconced in your crib back to Las Vegas in the morning."

Vance leaned back in anticipation of the ecstasy and release he was about to have. He needed this escape after finding out that Dwayne, who he had known his entire life, had been murdered just hours before. He could still see Dwayne lifting him up on his first pony. He wanted to cry, but he had to be strong. Instead, he moaned as she stroked and swalloed his manhood, causing his semen to explode into her mouth. Amazingly, she deep throated it all as if she were drinking a tall glass of milk.

Sitting up, Johnyce reached into her bag, pulled out a wipe, then popped several mints into her mouth.

"Well, I just tasted you, and I feel the same way. I don't know what it is, but it is as if I have been waiting for you my entire life. And my feelings are not just motivated by your money, Mr. Vance Dumas. There is also something about you that I really like. I would like the chance to see where this goes."

Vance laid her back on the long limousine seat, and made love to her. This was about to be the best ninety-minute ride from the Hamptons to the city he had ever experienced. For the first time in his life, he thought he might be falling in love.

CHAPTER SIXTEEN

Rome and Turquoise
Lust or True Love?

NOT WANTING to be caught up in Turquoise's never ending tangled web of deception, Rome asked her, "Do you want another drink? We need to make this fast. I don't have long to listen to your bullshit."

"I'll have a mimosa."

"You got that?" he asked the waiter.

"Yes, sir. I'll be right back with the lady's drink."

"Okay talk."

Turquoise reached out to touch Rome's hand, but he jerked it back.

"I said *talk,* not touch."

As soon as the waiter put the orange juice and champagne in front of her, Turquoise took a long sip.

"It's simple, darling. I hate myself for what I did to you. I still cannot believe that I let myself fall under Royale, I mean Rolondo's spell. I guess the excitement of having two rich and handsome men in love with me gassed up my ego. I got greedy. I wanted you both. I have been in therapy now for a long time. I have changed. I love you! Please take me back."

Rome could not believe his body was betraying him. His manhood was getting hard looking at and listening to Turquoise's voice. Prior to meeting her at Ralph's Market in Los Angeles, although he was a professional football player, Rome had only been with one woman, Davida. He had experienced sexual moves with Turquoise he never dreamed about. He would be lying to himself if he said he did not miss the bedroom action of their relationship. Amethyst was sexy, but she wasn't Turquoise in the sack. The woman sitting in front of him used to make his toes curl!

"I don't know whether you, my son, or his mother, Davida, hurt me the most. She cheated on me from the beginning when we met at the University of California Los Angeles, and then married a doctor she was seeing behind my back years later. I fell in love with you. I asked you to marry me. And all the while you were fucking that criminal clown whenever you were not with me. I treated you like you were a queen. I will admit I still have feelings for you. But I am going to tread lightly about rekindling anything with you. I have been seeing Amethyst for quite some time now. I am not ready to end that relationship yet. She is a lovely woman. However, against my better judgement, I do not see why we can't have dinner from time to time."

Tears trickled down Turquoise's face. She regretted making that pact with Sincere. She vowed to tell him she was no longer down for his wicked game of thievery.

"Thank you, my darling. I love you so much. I have one more favor to ask. Do you think that you can arrange for me to talk to Valerie? I would like to start over with her. I promise to put my petty jealousy of her behind me."

"Yes," said Rome. "I'll speak to her. She may not go for it

though. You have been rough on her through the years. So, are you heading back to Los Angeles?"

"No, I want to be near you. I am still an outpatient at the clinic in Southampton. I made a lot of money from selling Victor the compound for Valerie. In fact, there is a house that I've been asked to sell in Southampton that I can actually live in until I find a buyer for it."

Rome signaled for the waiter.

"Please give the lady another drink."

He continued. "I have to get back to Valerie's. Amethyst is there waiting for me. I will talk to Amethyst about us. As I said, I'm not ready to end things with her yet. For now, I will just roll the dice and see where life falls. Are you sure that is okay with you?"

"It has to be," said Turquoise. "I have really missed being with you. After I behaved so badly, I'm just grateful you are willing to give me another chance. So where do we go from here?"

Rome put three one hundred-dollar bills on the table to cover Turquoise's drinks, and anything else she might want. He stood up, then bent down, kissing her lightly on the lips.

"I'll call you. Take care of yourself."

As he walked out of the door, he did not see Valerian sitting in a dark corner at the bar where he had seen their conversation. As soon as he was sure Rome had left the hotel, he joined Turquoise at her table.

"Damn, baby, you sure know how to work it. You must have put a hurting on that lame motherfucker when you were together. He believed everything that you said, hook, line, and sinker."

"I was telling him the truth, Sincere. I do not know what I was thinking earlier. Our deal is off. I refuse to be part of your scheme to destroy Rome or Valerie. I am in love with him. If he gives me another chance, I want to do things right this time."

Before Valerian could respond, a man, Turquoise assumed to be Royale came back into the restaurant. Turquoise looked at him with awe. Although he had just left fifteen minutes ago, he had changed into a dark purple suit, lavender shirt, and purple tie. He had also gotten a haircut as well. Most surprisingly, Sincere stood up and hugged him.

Said Rafael, "I'm sorry that I just got here Sincere. I was able to spend some time with Claude to prepare him for the meeting with the lawyer in the morning before his arraignment."

At the sight of Rafael, chills ran up and down Turquoise's spine. Fearing everyone was lying, and Rolondo was still alive, she addressed her worries.

"I feel like I'm living in the twilight zone. A little while ago, you just left here with Valerie, wearing an entirely different outfit with long hair. Your voice is even different. Are you Rolondo?"

With his usual sinister laugh, Sincere told her, "Forgive me my bronze beauty. May I introduce you to my cousin, Rafael? His resemblance to his dear departed brother, Rolondo, and our lame duck cousin, Royale, is. . . shall I say, quite uncanny, isn't it? Rafael, this is Turquoise Hobson."

"The pleasure is all mine. I admit people used to think we were triplets," laughed Rafael. "But the women always told me I was the finer one. So, I presume that Royale must have also been here. I am sorry that I missed him."

"I told him that you had been released from prison and were heading here. However, I have plans for you and Valerie Rollins, who is now Royale's fiancé. But we will talk about that later."

Valerian turned his attention to Turquoise.

He moved in close to her, whispering, "You are not getting out of any deal. I can have you killed the moment you get up from this table. You are going to do exactly what we discussed, you hear me? Now go upstairs and wait for me while I talk to my cousin. One more thing, if you utter one word to Rome about what I just told Rafael about Valerie; I will kill both of you. Do you understand me, bitch? I am not Rome, Rolondo, or Yohance. Do not fuck with me!"

She jumped up and backed away from the table. Turquoise reached out to take the money Rome had left, only to have Sincere swat her hand away.

"I don't think so. Even high-class hoes like you always have to pay Daddy. Now get out of here."

Turquoise made a hasty exit from the restaurant. Instead of going to her room, she walked right out of the hotel, leaving her belongings upstairs, then proceeded to get into one of the taxis standing outside.

"Please take me to Kennedy Airport."

She was taking the next flight to Las Vegas. It would be easy for her to disappear in the world of casinos and fluff. She could always buy new clothes and rent an anonymous apartment, but her life was not for sale. Getting back with Rome was put on hold for now. Viva Las Vegas!

CHAPTER SEVENTEEN

Sincere and Rafael
Six Degrees of Separation

"I SEE that you are still up to your old tricks, Sincere. What was that all about," asked Rafael?

"She is one of your brother's ex-girlfriends. She crossed him, so we set her up to be turned out. But then Rolondo was killed."

"I see, and what do you mean that you have plans for Valerie Rollins and me? I do not want to do anything to harm Royale's relationship with that woman. I remember he was in love with her when he was in college. You did everything you could to break them up even back then. Before we thought Royale was dead, he was the only one of you who put money on my books while I was inside. In fact, the only reason I have money now is because he put fifty thousand dollars in my prison account. The warden gave it to me the day I was released."

"Don't tell me you went straight in prison. Do you want to order something to eat?"

"Yes, I went straight. I am no longer in the life. I have no plans to ever get locked up again. So, you can count me out of any of your schemes. To answer your second question, no, I do not have time to eat. I am just here to pick up the key to Claude's safe deposit box from you so that I can get cash out for his bail hearing tomorrow and to pay the lawyer. I'm also trying to catch up with a woman whose name is Amethyst Printup. She has been living in that house Rolondo bought in Harlem for years. Claude says the deed to it is also in the safe deposit box. I am Rolondo's next of kin and have no place to live right now, so I plan to move into the house. I went by there earlier today, but no one answered the door."

"I have the answer to all of your problems," said Sincere. "Amethyst is at Valerie's house. She has been dating Rome Nyland for three years. Your favorite cousin, Royale, is also there."

"Rome Nyland who used to play football? This Amethyst chick gets around."

"She always has. I will call our cousin right now."

Sincere pulled out his phone and punched up Royale.

"What do you want now, Sincere?" asked Royale.

"Someone wants to speak to you," Sincere told him, handing Rafael the phone.

"Hey, Royale. This is Rafael. How are you?"

"I'm great, cousin. Welcome home. What I do not understand, though, is why you reached out to Sincere after he ruined your life."

"I am just trying to help Claude. He never did anything to me. Sincere has something that Claude needs for court tomorrow. I just came to collect it. Listen, Sincere says a woman named Amethyst Printup is with you?"

"Amethyst is not with me, but she is staying on my fiancé's property for a few days with her boyfriend, Rome Nyland. He works with Valerie and lives here. Why are you interested in Amethyst's whereabouts?"

"She has been living in a house that Rolondo owns in Harlem for years. I'm his next of kin and I plan to move in there. I need to come over there and speak with her."

Royale could not believe what Rafael told him. He didn't know Amethyst had been hooked up with Rolondo.

"This is some pretty shocking news. Let me speak to Valerie and I will call you right back. Do you have a cell phone number so I don't have to go through our cousin?"

"Yes," said Rafael. "It is 312-555-5055. What is your number?"

"917-555-4826. Talk to you in a minute."

Royale did a mad dash into Val's office, where she was just finishing up her calls and her show.

"Baby, I'm sorry to disturb you, but my cousin, Rafael, just called me and blew my mind with the information he laid on me."

"Nothing surprises me with your family. What kind of information did he have?"

"He told me that Amethyst was hooked up with Rolondo and the house she lives in is in his name. Rafael wants to move in there now that he is out of prison. I guess Sincere told him that she is here, so he wants to come over to talk to her. Do you think that could be true?"

"Yes, I do. I have always had my suspicions about Amethyst. I even thought it was weird the way Rome met her on a flight and the next minute, they were practically insepara-ble. And I never understood how she could afford to live in that multi-level brownstone working part-time, teaching ice skating.

She never seems to be on duty at a hospital as a nurse. Do you trust your cousin Rafael?"

"Yeah, baby. I do. He is not like Rolondo, Sincere, or Claude. He was only a teenager when he took the fall for Rolondo and Sincere. They thought he would be sent to a juvenile facility, but the district attorney tried him as an adult since he was eighteen at the time. You know on Sunday, I noticed that Claude and Sincere exchanged a look between each other when Rome mentioned Amethyst's name while he was on the phone with her. I had a hunch something was up. I am sorry I did not mention that incident to you. I won't sleep on any more possible information that I might obtain."

"That's all right. So much goes on from one second to the next around here, that you can get dizzy trying to decipher it all. Call Rafael back and tell him to come over. I will call Rome and tell him to meet us in the library and to bring Amethyst. I do not know who has the worst luck with women, Rome or Vance. Help me, God!"

Val pressed the button on the intercom to Rome's house.

"Hey, what's up?" asked Rome.

"We may have a problem. Royale's cousin, Rafael, just called him because he is looking for Amethyst. Valerian told him she is here, and he wants to come by to speak with her."

"How does he know Amethyst?"

"Rafael says Rolondo owns the house she is living in and since he is the next of kin, he wants to live there now that he is out of prison," said Val.

"That doesn't make any sense. She told me that she inherited the house from a man she once knew. But she never told me his name. Well, now I know. It looks like his name was Rolondo Jemison."

Val told him, "Meet me in the library with Amethyst. Royale says this Rafael is all right, so he is headed here. In the meantime, I am going to do a background check on Amethyst to see what she was doing between 1980 and 2016 when you met this chick."

Rome told Val, "We'll see you in about ten minutes." He hung up the phone and went into the bedroom where Amethyst was getting dressed.

He told her, "I truly hope the information that Val just shared with me about you is not true."

Although she wasn't sure what Val had on her, eventually Amethyst knew her dark past would come to light. Playing dumb would be the best course to take at this point.

"What did Ms. Legendary Gossip Columnist have to say about me?"

"Where did this attitude you suddenly have with Valerie come from? She says that the house you live in belongs to the deceased Rolondo Jemison and that his brother, Rafael, has been released from prison and is looking for you. He plans to move into the house. Except for Royale, you know all the problems we have with that family. If you were once hooked up with Rolondo, why did you keep it a secret from me?"

Putting her arms around Rome's neck, tears started flowing. Amethyst answered, "I could not tell you, Rome. I did not want you to know about my past once I retired from ice skating professionally. All that dreadful stuff between Rolondo and me happened so long ago. After I had the accident, I became addicted to pain killers. I met Rolondo at his afterhours spot in South Central Los Angeles. He soon turned me on to heroin, and then turned me out. It took me years to get clean. I moved to New York, and he followed me here. He had so much dirt on me. I married my husband to get away from Rolondo, but then Manny died. I had nowhere to go so I started working for Rolondo again, then moved into his house. Then he was killed, and I have been quietly living there for the last four years. I may as well come totally clean. I also know Sincere and Claude, and I knew one day I would be put out of that house because I have no legal documents pertaining to it. Please don't leave me, darling."

"I cannot believe this shit keeps happening to me with you women. I can't even look at you. You are a despicable liar and a fraud. I want you out of my sight as soon as possible. But right now, we are going up to the house to let Val know what really went down."

"All right," said Amethyst. "I will do whatever you want me to do. I love you and don't want to lose you."

* * *

Back at the hotel, Rafael's phone rang.

"Yes, Royale?"

"Hey. My fiancé says it is all right for you to come over here to speak to Amethyst. I just texted you the address. How are you traveling around?"

"Two of Claude's ladies from the church are driving me. "

"Okay, we're in Bridgehampton, which isn't too far from where you are. I'll text you the address right away. It will be good to see you."

"It will be good to see you, too. It's been a long time," said Rafael.

He hung up and told Sincere, "Royale said to come over to Valerie's house and speak to Amethyst, so I need to get there as soon as possible. Can I get the safe deposit key now?"

Handing him a Louis Vuitton briefcase, Sincere told him, "It is in here along with twenty thousand dollars for you. This is my way of saying I am sorry for you spending most of your life in prison. I really should go over to Valerie's estate with you. I hate to miss all the fun that scene is going to be. But I have to go upstairs and deal with Turquoise."

"Cousin, don't you ever get tired of ruining and taking people's lives, stealing and constantly, wreaking havoc?" asked Rafael. "You guys are getting too old to keep doing all of these dastardly deals. It is time for you to get out of the game. You have more than enough money."

"That is where you are wrong," said Sincere. "No one can ever have too much money. But I am moving back to Switzerland as soon as I make the score I am working on now. I am tired of vipping and vopping between Los Angeles, New York City, and Sag Harbor."

Rafael stood up.

Patting the briefcase, he told Sincere, "Thanks for everything in here. I will call you tomorrow with an update on Claude after court. If he hadn't killed that FBI agent in cold blood in front of everyone, we could have gotten him out on bail. This is going to be a tough one."

"He was trying to kill Royale. I agree with you that shooting anyone with so many people around was just plain long stupid, but Claude has never been the smart one. I will speak to you tomorrow," said Sincere.

CHAPTER EIGHTEEN

Amethyst
Amethyst's Angst

Valerie slipped on a Dolce & Gabbana floral tulle ruched midi-dress and a pair of the design duo peep-toe mules for the meeting and dinner. The colors in the dress matched the pink diamond ring Royale gave her the night before. She had planned tonight's dinner to celebrate their engagement.

Now between, Dwayne's murder and discovering Amethyst was connected to the late Rolondo, her celebratory mood was gone.

"You certainly look beautiful, my love," said Royale, as they headed into the library. He had also changed into a beige linen suit, and was wearing the rare Dior Air Jordan 1 sneakers Val had given him for Christmas that retailed for twenty- three hundred dollars a pair. She also gifted Rome and Vance with them. Val had heard the shoes were now going for ten thousand dollars on a reseller site called Stock X.

"Thank you, darling. I was looking forward to a quiet evening to relish in the fact that I am finally marrying you. It is not every day you get the fairytale at sixty years old."

"You still look and have the spirit of any thirty-year-old woman!"

"Back at you, baby. You are like fine wine. You just keep getting better with time!"

* * *

Rome and Amethyst were seated in the library when Royale and Valerie walked in.

Books had always been the equivalent of fine jewelry to Val, so her library was spectacular. Aside from being a gossip columnist and radio host, she was the author of four best-selling novels as well. The two-story room was circular with soaring wooden shelves filled with almost one thousand first editions, as well as entire collections from all of Valerie's favorite authors which included the deceased E. Lynn Harris, James Baldwin, Eric Jerome Dickey, Jackie Collins, and the author whose work led her to New York City and the entertainment world, following her graduation from Howard University, Jacqueline Susann.

As well as Wahida Clark, Zane, Kimberla Lawson Roby, Carl Weber, Curtis Bunn, Danielle Steel, her friend La Toya Jackson's two books and an impressive collection from Fern Michaels. A gorgeous red velvet couch, matching love seat, built in bar, and a circa 1790 satinwood worktable sat in the middle of the perfect literary retreat.

This was the first time Amethyst had been invited into the luxurious room.

"This library is magnificent, Valerie. A true nerd's dream," she said dryly.

"I have never been accused of being a nerd," said Val. "But I have always been a bookworm. However, I did not bring you in here to discuss my love of books. I know we are all guilty of committing sins of omission, and I also realize that Rolondo has been dead for a while now. But it was extremely dangerous and deceptive of you not to reveal your affiliation with him to us. I just ran a criminal background check on you, which uncovered many arrests in Los Angeles, Las Vegas, and New York for prostitution. Each time, one of Royale's treacherous cousins bailed you out. No wonder you do not work as a nurse. With your record, you can never get a license. What do you want with Rome? Did they sic you on him?"

"No, they did not. Rome and my meeting on the flight from Los Angeles to New York was honestly coincidental. Rolondo was killed the week after I met Rome. I had no idea that Claude and Sincere were also on the east coast. I thought they were back in California. I fell in love with Rome. I will admit that I knew Rolondo was masquerading as Royale, but I never dreamed all of you were connected. I have also been naïve enough to convince myself that none of Rolondo's relatives would ever want my house or show up to claim it."

"Well, I am his only sibling, and I am here now to do just that," said Rafael as he walked through the door.

Royale hugged Rafael.

"You look great, cousin. Are you sure you weren't hibernating in some health club for thirty-five years instead of being in prison?"

"Only you would say that since we look just alike," laughed Rafael.

"He is right. You guys look more alike than you and Rolondo did, Royale," said Val.

Linking his arm through Valerie's, Royale said, "Rafael, this is my fiancé, Valerie Rollins, and this is Rome Nyland and his lady, Amethyst Printup."

Putting her arms around his shoulders, Val told Rafael, "I'm a hugger. It is genuinely nice to meet you, Rafael. Welcome to my home."

"Thank you so much for allowing me to come here. I feel like I just entered Buckingham Palace. It is also an honor to meet you, Mr. Nyland. I have been a fan of yours for most of my life. I wish I was here under better circumstances, Ms. Printup."

Shaking Rafael's hand, Rome said, "Please, call me Rome. I think I have a solution for the problem. Why don't we all have a seat?"

At that moment, Jonelle, accompanied by three servers, walked in with several serving carts filled with chicken wings, an assortment of cheese and crackers, and platters of vegetables and fruits. There was also a cart that held small plates, utensils, and napkins, as well as one with glasses and decanters of merlot and chardonnay, water, ginger ale, coca cola, cranberry, and orange juice on it.

"I thought you might be a little hungry or thirsty, guys. Such serious talk goes better with food and drinks. Help yourselves before we start. You're also welcome to stay for dinner, Rafael," said Val.

"Thank you. I have not had a chance to eat all day. I see why my cousin has been in love with you since he was twenty," said Rafael. He got up and fixed a plate and poured himself a glass of ginger ale.

Amethyst had been quiet up until now.

"What is going on in this room right now is ridiculous. This man is here to put me out of my home, and you are hosting a cocktail party, Valerie. The possibility of me losing my home is not something to celebrate."

"No one is celebrating anything. I am just trying to put everyone at ease, Amethyst. You got yourself into this mess. I am going to have a glass of wine and some wings because I have a feeling we aren't going to have dinner anytime soon."

"Here you are, Ms. Val," said Jonelle, as she set a plate in front of Valerie on the coffee table and handed her a glass of chardonnay.

Sitting down with his food, Rafael told Amethyst, "I am very sorry, but as you may know, I have been locked up since I was a teenager for a crime that I did not commit. I have no place to live, and I am Rolondo's next of kin, so I am going to have to ask you to leave the house."

"You can ask me anything you want to, but you are going to have to take me to court to get me out of there," snarled Amethyst.

"Now hold up, Amethyst," said Rome. "Rafael, do you know how much Rolondo paid for the house?"

"Yes, I do. Claude told me he bought it off some junkie whose mother left it to him for fifty thousand dollars in cash. He really was not interested in owning a house in Harlem, but it was too good of an opportunity for him to pass up."

Rome also knew a promising investment when he saw one. He had been wanting to own property in Harlem for quite some time.

"I have a proposition for you. The property value of a home in Harlem is worth a lot more than fifty thousand dollars in 2021," said Rome. "I am prepared to give you a cashier's check for three-hundred-thousand dollars if you sell the house to me and I will let Amethyst continue to live in the apartment on the top floor. I have helped her upgrade the brownstone by putting in a new kitchen, refurbishing three bathrooms, and having the basement completely redone. I would hate to just lose the place after we did so much work to improve it. I just had another epiphany. The basement apartment is unoccupied at the present time. It is a one bedroom. Since Royale says you got such a raw deal in life, I don't mind if you live in it rent free. We can make the transaction tomorrow. You can sign over the deed to me, while walking away with some nice change in your pocket, as well as a brand new place to live."

A startled Amethyst blurted out, "That sounds like the perfect arrangement to me. After all of this, you would really buy the house and let me still live in it, Rome?"

"I just made the man the offer, didn't I?"

"Yes, you did."

"What do you think, cousin?" asked Royale. "It sounds like a sweet deal to me."

"Although it does sound like music to my ears, the lawyer in me says I should speak to a real estate agent first, just to make sure the $300K is a fair offer for the property," said Rafael. "In the meantime, you are welcome to continue living there, Amethyst, and I will happily take Rome up on the offer to move into the apartment's basement. I am staying at the A-loft Hotel in Harlem tonight. It is also required that I check in with my parole officer tomorrow and start looking for a job. Even if I do come into all this money, the parole board will still demand that I am gainfully employed."

In between bites of a chicken wing, Royale told him, "You can work with me and my minor league baseball team, the Sag Harbor Scorpions. With your new law expertise, I will make you the director of operations. You were always a better player than I was anyway. You just let the lure of the streets get in the way of the sport."

"If you are going to be working with my future husband," said Val. "You are also welcome to stay one of our guest suites here."

"When I walked into this beautiful estate, I had no idea

this meeting would turn out like this. . . a huge real estate offer. . . a dream job. . . even temporary housing. I always knew how good of a guy you are, Royale. But I sure did not know you and Rome were such nice people, Valerie. Thank you, all, "said Rafael.

"Excuse me everyone," said Kahari, as he entered the room. "Rome, Valerian is at the gate. He says that he's looking for Ms. Turquoise."

"I swear that man has a habit of ruining any good time we seem to have. Why would he think Turquoise would be here?" asked Val.

"When I left him at the hotel, he said he was going upstairs to deal with Turquoise," offered Rafael. "She must have left before he got to the room."

"Kahari, let him come in," said Rome. "Then signal the other guys to be geared up just in case there is any trouble."

"You got it."

"I don't want to be a snitch," said Rafael. "But when I got to the hotel, Sincere was threatening Turquoise about going back to you, Rome. She told him that after talking things over with you, she wanted out of some deal the two of them had. He told her he would kill her first."

Amethyst yelled at Rome. "You were talking with your ex-girlfriend at the hotel? So that's why you did not come back with Royale and Valerie! How could you do that to me?"

"How could you do that to dear, sweet Amethyst, Rome," asked Valerian as he sauntered in. "Why Didn't you invite me to this party, Valerie? Starting tomorrow, I thought we were going to be friends at least until Friday."

Val rolled her eyes at him, shook her head, then pointed to the spread on the table.

"Feel free to help yourself to some appetizers and a drink, Valerian."

Ignoring Val and Valerian, Amethyst shouted at Rome. "You didn't answer me!"

"We can talk about this later in private, Amethyst. Valerian, why would you think that Turquoise would be here?" asked Rome.

Pouring himself a glass of chardonnay, and taking a seat next to Rafael, Valerian answered, "I really wish you people would start calling me Sincere. I overheard your little chat with Turquoise, about you willing to give your relationship another chance, but at the same time, you are not ready to end things with Amethyst. When I went up to her room, she was not there. Then the desk clerk at the hotel informed me that she left in a taxi. So, I assumed this was her destination. Turquoise and I have unfinished business to discuss."

"Well, Sincere, as you can see, Turquoise is not here. Now you can finish your drink and leave," said Royale.

"No, don't leave yet, Sincere. I want to hear more about my so-called man getting back together with that sleazy bitch," snarled Amethyst.

"Please calm down, Amethyst. Rome just offered to buy a three-hundred-thousand-dollars home and let you live in it rent free, so it is obvious the man loves you," said Val.

"Oh, shut up, you old fat cow. You think you are such hot shit with your billions of dollars and so many men always around you, but you are not. I hate you!"

With those words having spewed out of her mouth, Amethyst stood up, threw her drink into Val's face, then lunged at her.

Royale jumped up and pulled Amethyst away from Valerie.

"You need to get your woman under control, Rome!"

"I'm on it," answered Rome. He grabbed Amethyst's hand.

"It's time for us to go back to my house right this minute. Are you okay?" he asked Val.

"Just a little wet," she said, while wiping her face with a napkin. "I'll be fine."

"There you go again, only being concerned about her fat ass!" yelled Amethyst as Rome dragged her out of the library.

"I knew this was going to be too much fun to miss," sneered Valerian.

"Give me a break, Sincere," said Royale. "I don't know what has gotten into Amethyst, but you coming over here with your tell-all story about Rome and Turquoise certainly didn't help keep matters calm."

"Oh, forget you, cousin. I did them both a favor. Now he can just dump Amethyst and go crawling back to Turquoise. Everyone thinks Rome Nyland is some sort of a superhero, but he's really a pussy whipped fool."

"Stop talking about my best friend like that, Valerian. However, he does get caught up in his women. You are right about that," said Val. "You know, I halfway like your sinister sense of humor, and you look so much like Victor that I believe there might be a soul somewhere inside of your evil body. I took care of our business earlier, so expect a delivery at the hotel around noon. I have to speak to Vance on the other matter, but he hasn't answered his phone all evening."

"That's no surprise," said Sincere. "I'm sure Vance has been dick deep in the pretty minister's pussy ever since they left the hotel together this afternoon."

"Sincere, watch your mouth. There is a lady present," said Rafael.

"It's okay, Rafael. I'm getting used to his off color comments," said Val.

"Ga-Ga, I have been waiting for you all day," said Valencia, as she ran into the room, dressed in a plaid Burberry dress, with matching sneakers. She flew into Val's arms.

"Hey my darling, granddaughter!"

Valencia looked from Royale to Rafael in confusion.

"Mr. Royale, there are two of you!"

"Not really, sweetheart. This is my cousin, Mr. Rafael. We just look a lot alike."

"You sure do!"

She then looked curiously at Valerian.

"You look like my grandfather, but he died."

"I know he passed away," said Sincere. "He was my older brother. I am your other grandfather. Your

mother, Violet, was my daughter."

Valencia turned her attention to Valerie.

"Ga-Ga, do I have another grandfather?"

Although Valerie hadn't planned to tell Valencia about her mother's father, and she also didn't like the fact Valerian was in the same room with Valencia, against her better judgement she decided to tell the little girl the truth.

"Yes, sweetheart, you do. This is Valerian. As he just told you, he is your mother's father."

Before Val could grab her, Valencia walked over to Valerian and kissed him on the cheek.

"It's nice to meet you, Grandfather."

"I'm glad to meet you too, little one."

Valerian stood up.

"It's time for me to go. I look forward to hearing from you tomorrow, Valerie. Cousins, goodnight. I'll speak to you tomorrow, Rafael."

"I'll walk out with you, Sincere. It is time I got back to the city. Thank you for everything, Valerie and Royale. I am happy to see you two finally together after all these years. Congratulations on your upcoming marriage."

"Thank you," said Val. "Kahari will see you both out."

Valerian turned around and looked at Val before he left.

"Don't think I'm getting soft or starting to like you, Valerie. However, thank you for telling Valencia that she is also my granddaughter. You do not have to worry any longer. I will make sure no harm ever comes her way. I cannot believe these words are coming out of my mouth, but I am starting to see why my dearly departed brother married you, and this lame duck cousin of mine has always loved you. You are doing a good job with Valencia. But you better still watch your back when it comes to me."

"I got your lame duck, Sincere," said Royale.

"Goodnight, Valerian. We will talk on Friday," said Valerie.

"Right this way, gentlemen," said Kahari.

Valerie pulled Royale and Valencia close to her as the men left.

"Baby, go to the dining room with Nanny. Royale and I will be there soon."

"Okay, Ga-Ga!"

Holding Val tightly, Royale asked, "What do you think got into Amethyst to make her go so crazy?"

"It had to be a pretty big shock hearing that Rome is contemplating going back to Turquoise. But I do not know why Amethyst took that out on me. She should have thrown the wine in Rome's face, not mine."

Royale laughed.

"Do you think he will still buy Rolondo's house and let her stay there?"

"Yes, I do. Rome is not the type of man to go back on his word. This day has been too much. A man, that I cared about, was shot dead right in front of me. I still cannot believe this morning really happened. I am exhausted and I still have not had a chance to look through Dwayne's room to see if we can find any clues to who may have put a hit out on him."

"Leave that for tomorrow. You need to get some rest. Why don't we sit with Valencia for a few minutes while she eats, then call it a night?" asked Royale.

"You got it, sweetheart. That sounds like a master plan to me."

CHAPTER NINETEEN

Rome and Amethyst
Love On the Rocks

Not knowing whether to be angry or embarrassed about tossing a drink in Valerie's face, then trying to choke her, Amethyst poured herself a glass of merlot when she walked through the door of Rome's house.

"What happened back there?" asked Rome.

"I should be asking you the same thing. Why are you contemplating going back to Turquoise? I thought we have a good thing going on."

"I felt we were grooving together pretty well too. But you have been a different person this weekend, Amethyst. You seem to like Valerie and get along with her. But since yesterday, you've been making snide remarks about her. And do not think I haven't noticed the way you look at Royale. Is that your problem? Do you want to trade me in for him? Because that will never happen. That man loves Val's last year's dirty panties."

"No, I do not want to trade you in for him. I guess I'm just curious about him because he looks so much like Rolondo. I was very vulnerable during the time he had me in his clutches. Now, with Rafael on the scene, I see there are three of them. They must have drove the women crazy when they were young."

"They may have done just that. However, from what I hear, and have been seeing for the last four years, is that from the time they were teenagers, Royale only had eyes for Val. I have watched the way he looks at her, as if she is a piece of gold and the most beautiful woman on earth."

"I've noticed that too," said Amethyst. "I guess between both of you being so devoted to Valerie, combined with this unbelievable estate she owns; I have become very resentful of her. How can one woman have so much? But that is all beside the point. Did you really tell Turquoise you all are getting back together?"

"I told her I would think about it," admitted Rome. "I was engaged to the woman. I do still have feelings for her, but I also care a lot about you. Honestly, today, you have both disappointed me. Between Rafael telling us she has something going on with Valerian, and you being so involved with his family, and not telling me, maybe I need to take a break from both of you. Plus, my friend was murdered this morning. I can't waste any more time today with this drama. I need to look through Dwayne's phone right now, then go up to the main house and look through his suite so I can find out who was behind his death. At this moment, that is where my concentration needs to be. This relationship drama will have to wait."

Placing her hand on Rome's, Amethyst told him, "I can understand that. I am sorry about everything. I should have told you about my history with Rolondo. I will also apologize to Valerie for saying those nasty things to her and throwing the drink in her face. But I'm not ready to give you up, Rome. I love you."

"Like I just said, I need to concentrate on who killed Dwayne. For once, I think Valerian is telling the truth about him and Claude not being involved in his murder. I also need to line up some extra security for Vance's trip to Texas tomorrow. Why don't you pack up your things and I'll call an Uber to take you back to the city? I will touch base with Rafael tomorrow about buying the house. Right now, we need a little distance from each other though."

Amethyst could not believe what she was hearing come out of Rome's mouth.

"No, I'm not ready to go back to the city alone tonight. Please don't throw me out like I am a bag of trash!"

"All right. All right. I will be in my office taking care of some things for a couple of hours. You can go home in the morning."

With those parting words, Rome walked out of the living room. As he left, Amethyst whispered, "You can't fool me with a house or letting me stay here one more night. I know this relationship is over. Sorry, Rome, but I can't go back to my old life."

Amethyst opened her purse and took out a vial of pills she had been taking all day, then poured herself a large glass of merlot to wash them down. Refilling her glass, she headed to the kitchen, grabbed a huge sharp knife, then went to the bathroom where she ran a warm bath. Once she was in the tub, she took the knife and made a small incision on her right wrist, then leaned back to accept whatever her fate was. It was either kill Rome, Turquoise or herself. It had to be her because death outweighed sitting in a prison cell for murder.

CHAPTER TWENTY

Vance and Johnyce
When Lust Meets Love

"All right everyone, it was a great party. Tell Mary good-night for me," Vance told the owner of the Brooklyn Chop House, as he and Johnyce exited the popular restaurant in New York City's Financial District.

Robert "Don Pooh" Cummings was a music industry impresario and longtime friend of Mary J. Blige.

The name of the restaurant was a play on both a meat chop and chopsticks, which one of Don Pooh's business partners, Stratis Morfogen, told Forbes Magazine. "There might not be a restaurant on earth that can serve a four-pound salt and pepper lobster, alongside a fifty-five-day prime dry-aged Porterhouse steak and a seven-pound slow roasted Peking duck, but that's what sets our restaurant apart."

"That was incredible," said Johnyce, as she and Vance slid into the back of the limousine. "I cannot believe I was in the same room that Mary J. Blige was in, and her Sun Goddess wine is delicious. So was the food. Thank you for taking me, Vance. Thank you for everything."

Not being able to control himself, Vance caressed her breasts and kissed her.

"You are very welcome, doll. There is no reason not to keep this party going. Do you want to come to Texas with me tomorrow? You have helped me a lot today to not think about my friend, Dwayne, who was more like an uncle to me, being killed this morning. I was going to postpone the trip, but Dwayne would want me to keep on doing business as usual."

Johnyce told him, "I would love to come with you. I have never been to Texas, and I am really enjoying being in your company. You are a very genuine guy. People really like you, and it is not because you are so wealthy and famous. I could tell that everyone was very happy to see you."

"So, the question is how much is it going to cost me? Name your price, baby."

"Okay, my price is that we make it a real date rather than a trick. I do not want any more of your money. I simply want to hang with you and get to know you better. I cannot understand it, but I feel like I've known you all of my life."

"You are the first woman I have ever met that has turned down money that I offered her. We may not have known each other our entire lives, but I am glad as hell you are in my life now," said Vance, as he devoured Johnyce's breasts with kisses.

"Vance," whispered Johnyce.

"Yes, sweet one?"

"Don't get it twisted. I did take your money earlier, and I am happy to keep all of it. But from here on out, I do not want this relationship to be transactional. I would like to find out what having true feelings for someone is about. I have never been in a real relationship. The streets are the only life I have known since I was sixteen. Do you think you can do that? I mean, we all read the tabloids. Your reputation with women is pretty wild."

"Hey, I'm not trying to brag, but most of the risqué stuff you read and hear about me is true. I have always been a hit and quit it kind of guy who likes to have fun. But I am going through some real personal changes now. Every day I find out something new about my family, and who I really may be. I didn't even know I had cousins. Now they are coming out of the woodwork, and I really like Royale. He has become like a father to me. All of this is causing me to reevaluate my life. I could use a real woman in my corner, and for some reason, I think God dropped you down from the heavens into my lap today. Are you really an ordained minister?"

"Yes, I am," answered Johnyce. "After Pastor Claude rescued me off the streets of New York, he even got me into the Howard University School of Divinity. Although I will admit he made me work at The Camelot Showbar Strip Club on M Street NW the entire time I was in school. I gave all the money I made to him. I was so grateful to him that it didn't matter."

Slowly dipping his finger in and out of her vagina, Vance asked, "Is being a former stripper how you are acquainted with the twins and Ashro?"

Moaning as Vance's fingers stroked her, Johnyce told him, "Sort of. But the way I really know them is they also used to work for Pastor Claude."

Startled by that information, Vance sat up straight.

"You have got to be kidding."

"No, I am not. They may still work for him. And even though Sincere and I have never met before today, I have certainly heard Pastor Claude on the phone with him many times. You need to know that he does not mean you any good at all. Please be careful when it comes to both Sincere and Pastor Claude."

Vance replied, "Thank you. You really are an angel sent to me from heaven. We are already at the exit. We are back in the Hamptons. I do not want to spend this night without you. We can swing by the church in Sag Harbor and Raymond can drive your car. Stay with me tonight, and we'll head to Texas early in the morning."

"I need to go home to pack a bag. Also, as I told Valerie this morning, my identification didn't fit into this tiny Judith Leiber clutch, so it is a must that I pick up a larger purse. Plus, what is your in-house harem going to have to say when they see me? I don't want them to get any ideas about me joining in with their sexcapades!"

"I don't care about what they think. They are employed by me. We are flying on my plane, so you won't need your identification. You also do not have to worry about clothes. You look like you are a size four. I just so happen to have closets full of women's clothes, lingerie, shoes, and purses from every top designer at my house in every size. A true player like me is always prepared. I can't have any woman leaving my lair doing the walk of shame the next morning. I'll even throw in a brand new Louis Vuitton suitcase for you to pack it all in. This is your lucky day, baby because from now on, you are going to start living Vance Dumas style!"

"I am sure that Vance Dumas style is a wonderful way to live, but I want to travel in my own clothes, and lingerie, and I am not leaving town without identification. I also own my own Louis Vuitton suitcase to pack everything in. So, we need to swing by the church and pick up my car. It will not take me long to pull what I need together. Then, we will head back to your lair. Does that plan work for you?"

Kissing her on the neck, Vance said, "You really are different. Any plan you have to offer works for me, baby!"

CHAPTER TWENTY-ONE

Amethyst and Rome
A Life Worth Living

Rome texted Vance to let him know two armed guys from Hamptons Protection Group would be at his house in the morning to go with him to Texas. Rome then went to work, unlocking Dwayne's phone. Since Dumas Electronics paid for the employees' phones, Rome had everyone's passwords and social security numbers. So, getting into Dwayne's phone was not going to be a problem. Surprisingly, Dwayne did not have a passcode on the phone. Rome looked through his recent calls. The only calls in the past few days had been to him, Valerie, Kahari, Kwami, and Vance.

Next, he looked at his text messages. This was a different scenario because there were quite a few.

The first was to a 702-555-1493 number.

Dwayne:

I will not kill anyone for you. I have never been in jail and at fifty-five years old, I have no intention of getting locked up for the rest of my life. I did not rescue you eight years ago to be your lackey for life.

702-555-1493:

You had better do what I tell you to do. It is in your best interest to kill Sincere before he finds out you saved my life and have known that I was still alive all these years. Otherwise, he is going to kill you faster than a New York minute.

Dwayne:

No, when you get out of the hospital on Monday, you need to contact Sincere and tell him that you are alive. You should also tell your child the truth. You also have a granddaughter that it would be nice for you to get to know.

702-555-1493:

I will do no such thing. And you know I could never stand that spoiled ass kid of mine, nor do I have any intention of getting to know his child. That is definitely not going to happen.

Dwayne:

Then I guess I will have to tell Sincere myself that you are still among the living.

702-555-1493:

Try it, Dwayne, and you may as well have just signed your death warrant.

Dwayne:

I may not know a lot of things, but the one thing I do know is that you would never kill me. You cannot kill shit.

702-555-1493:

You had better do what I say, or you will soon be pushing up daisies. Have a good night!

Rome dialed the unknown number.

"This is Verizon Wireless. You have reached a disconnected number. Please check the number and dial it again."

Next, he called his main contact at Verizon, but got his

voicemail. He then punched in Val's number. As usual, she picked up on the first ring.

"Hey, how are things going over there? Did Amethyst calm down?"

"She calmed down, but I told her I need some distance from her and Turquoise. She wasn't too happy about that. But that's not why I called you. I looked through Dwayne's texts messages. Someone in Las Vegas has been threatening to kill him if Dwayne didn't kill Valerian."

"What?"

"You heard me. According to the text messages, Valerian thinks whoever this person is died. Dwayne told whoever they are, if they did not tell Sincere that they were still alive, he would. I cannot figure out if he was texting a man or a woman. I called the number, but it has already been disconnected. I called my guy at Verizon to see if he can trace who owns the phone but got his voicemail."

Val told Rome, "It's Sunday night. He is probably out to dinner. With all the crap Valerian keeps going on day and night, it is no surprise to me that someone wants him dead. I could care less if this person is trying to put him in his grave, but give him a call and see if he knows anything now that the tide has turned and now his low life ass is in danger. I will also let Royale know what is going on with his cousin. Are you coming back up here to grab some dinner? The kitchen staff hasn't put the food away yet."

"With everything that happened today, I had forgotten about eating. You ain't said nothing but a word. I am starving! I will grab Amethyst and be right up to the house. She also mentioned to me that she would like to apologize to you for her actions earlier."

"Oh Lord. Okay, hurry up. Royale and I are ready to call it

a night. I am glad you are on the way to finding out who would want to kill our friend. Thank you," said Valerie.

"It's all in a day's work, baby girl. See you in a few minutes."

Rome hung up the phone, then turned the lights out in his office.

"Amethyst," he called out. "Do you want to go back up to the main house and have dinner before it gets any later?"

She did not answer him.

"Amethyst, where are you?"

Rome checked his bedroom. She was not in there. He heard water running in the bathroom from the hallway.

He knocked on the door.

"Amethyst, baby, are you taking a bath?"

There was silence. As Rome stood there, water seeped from under the door, and covered his shoes.

Rome turned the doorknob, but the door was locked from the inside. He stepped back, then kicked the door open with his Timberland boots, with such force he almost fell into the bathtub which Amethyst was lying in with bleeding wrists.

He also noticed a half empty bottle of Oxycodone pills on the sink.

In one quick move, Rome turned off the faucet, then lifted her out of the tub. Putting his hand to her neck, he felt a pulse. He also could see the wound on her wrist was superficial, so he grabbed two hand towels off the rack and wrapped them fast. Luckily, there was a landline telephone on the wall in the bathroom. He dialed 9-1-1.

"My name is Rome Nyland. Please send an ambulance to one seventy-nine Maple Lane in Bridgehampton. I have a possible suicide attempt victim here. Her name is Amethyst Printup."

Forcing Amethyst to start walking, Rome practically dragged her with him back to his bathroom.

He kept an emergency medic bag and pulled out a syringe with Naloxone in it. He had been keeping this ever since Violet overdosed back in 2016. When he found her if he had been in possession of the Naloxone back then, the talented horse jockey may still have been alive today.

Rome gave Amethyst the injection. Her eyes slowly opened.

"I can't live without you, Rome. Please let me die," she moaned.

"I can't do that, baby."

The paramedics arrived fifteen minutes later. Led by Valerie and Royale, who Rome had forgotten to call to let them know what had just gone down, and that an ambulance was headed to the estate, they all burst into the house together.

"Rome, what happened? Why didn't you call me?" yelled Val.

"It all happened so fast. Amethyst tried to commit suicide."

He then told the paramedic, "She's going to need stitches on her wrist, but she just scratched the surface. It looks like she took some Oxycodone, but as you can see, she is awake now."

"Okay, thank you, sir. We have it from here," said the female medic. Picking up Amethyst's left arm, she told her, "Miss, let me wrap your wrist properly please, until we get you to the hospital and get you stitched up. Why would you want to harm yourself?"

Refusing to answer or even speak, Amethyst just continued crying loudly.

The paramedic then asked Rome, "How are you related to this woman, sir?"

"She's my girlfriend," said Rome.

"Can you tell us what happened?"

"We've had a challenging day, so I suggested that we give each other a little space. I went into my office to do some work. When I came out a little while later, I found her in the tub like this."

Royale whispered to Val, "We should go back up to the house and let them have some privacy."

Val agreed with him.

"Rome," said Val. "We should go back up to the house so the paramedics can work, all right? Let me know what I can do to help."

"Okay."

Val kissed Amethyst on the cheek.

"Get well real soon, okay? Royale and I are praying for you."

Wearily, Amethyst told Val, "I am so sorry about all of this."

Val grabbed Royale's hand, quickly leaving the house. Val was glad this horrific day was ending.

CHAPTER TWENTY-TWO

A Sizzling Sin City
Aurora and Jermonna
Late Monday Afternoon

CLAD in a blue denim Gucci monogrammed two-piece pants suit with a matching Dionysus shoulder bag and face mask, Jermonna Bradley was having a glass of champagne at the Vista Cocktail Lounge at Caesars Palace in Las Vegas. Her career started as a rapper. Back then, she went by the name of J'Body. One of her music videos caught the eye of Peter Unger, the producer of the nighttime drama Baldwin Hills. She cast as a zany assistant to the lead character, Shelby. Jermonna's character was Tiffany. Ironically, like actress Tiffany Haddish, Jermonna grew up in the foster care system. Unlike the Girls Trip star, she couldn't handle the fame, attention, and money that came along with being a celebrity. So, she became an uncontrollable Hollywood hellion. Trying to distance herself from the reputation she had in her twenties and thirties, of being the original Black industry wild television star, Jermonna was now a cast member on the reality show, *For The Love of WAGS* (*Wives and Girlfriends of High-Profile Athletes*). After years of hopping from man-to-man, she was engaged to Bartimaeus Sanford, a running back for the Detroit Lions. They met at former Heavyweight Champion Larry Holmes' Golf Tournament in Easton, Pennsylvania. Larry's wife, Diane, had invited Jermonna at the suggestion of gossip columnist, Flo Anthony, who went to the tournament every year with former Light Heavyweight/Heavyweight Champion of the World, Michael Spinks. Since they were both in the gossip game, Flo was very tight with Jermonna's best friend, Valerie Rollins.

Jermonna's on the edge lifestyle may have wreaked havoc on her acting career, but she was an ace at golf, who could have been in the PGA Tour. It was love at first sight for her and Bartimaeus when they met two years ago. Flo Anthony had also helped her to get her gig on *For The Love of WAGS*. Flo was offered a spot on the show, but was not interested, so she called Val to suggest Jermonna.

Bartimaeus had been all for her doing the show, and he also made some appearances on it. Their engagement and planning of the wedding became the show's main storyline. She was now in Vegas, filming her bachelorette weekend with the other girls.

Work had just ended for the day, so she was having some much needed alone time at the bar until her solace was interrupted by some loud voices. Although she could not see the ladies sitting in a booth near the bar, Jermonna could hear their entire conversation because they were practically shouting.

"Girl, now that you have finally recovered from all of those bullets being shot into your face and body, after all these years, you need to get your pussy tightened so you can hook up with a young guy. I had a vaginal rejuvenation, and I am back in the life, making big bucks. You do not need the money, so just do it to have fun," said one woman.

"Georgette, after being first in the hospital, and then at the rehabilitation home for eight years, then undergoing all those procedures I needed, just to come back to normal life, forget that, girl. I am never going under the knife again for anything or anyone. If I can still fuck, I'm sure my kitty cat will be just fine."

The second voice sounded familiar to Jermonna. She could not place it though, so she turned around to see who these women were. Jermonna almost went into shock when she saw the face the voice belonged to. She was looking straight at a ghost. She did not know whether to scream, run, or approach the woman. She didn't have to do either because the woman looked her dead in the eyes, got up from her chair, and approached her right away.

"Hello, Jermonna. Your habits never seem to change. The last time I ran into you was at this very same bar. And eight years later, you are still sitting here."

"Andrea, how can you still be alive? I was with you when you were killed. I heard all the shots and then someone shot me."

"My name is Aurora now. It is none of your business how I am still among the living. All you need to know is just like when a reporter told Mark Twain that his obituary had ran in a newspaper, the legendary writer said to that man, *'the reports of my death are greatly exaggerated.'* Now, forget you saw me in here, and if you want to stay alive, you had better keep your mouth shut. I may not be dead, but if you tell anyone you crossed paths with me, you will be!"

"Andrea, we were always friends. We used to party together like there was no tomorrow. I am happy to see that you are alive! Why are you threatening my life?" asked a now terrified Jermonna.

"First of all, we were never friends. I just hung around you because you always brought the good coke and the fine men. I do not want anyone to know I am still alive until I am good and ready. But right now, your biggest worry should be changing your pants," laughed Aurora.

The shock of seeing Andrea alive after so many years of believing she was dead, then being threatened by her, had caused Jermonna to pee in her pants. The urine gushed down around her designer shoes. She grabbed her purse from the bar and ran off to find the nearest bathroom.

Aurora sat back down with Georgette, then took a long sip of her Billecart-Salmon vintage champagne.

"There is no way that simple little bitch is going to keep her mouth shut."

"You want me to take care of her?" asked Georgette. "Just like back in the day, I have my trusty box cutter right in my purse. I never leave home without it!"

"Yes, I think you had better handle this situation. Meet me over at the suite at the Wynn. I will pay you ten-grand in cash like I used to when you did this kind of job for me. She should be in the nearest bathroom trying to get herself together," said Aurora.

"You got it, girl!"

With no further words, in a flash, the two women left the bar, heading in different directions.

After running into the bathroom, right outside of the bar, Jermonna was in a stall, trying to wipe her pants dry with paper towels. Luckily, her top was long enough to cover up the back of her pants until she could catch a quick cab over to the Venetian where she was staying. But right now, it was urgent for her to call Val and tell her that Andrea was still alive.

She punched up Val's number right away. To her dismay, the call went straight to voicemail.

"Hey Val, it's Jermonna. Please call me right away. You are

not going to believe who I just ran into at Caesars Palace in Vegas. This is urgent. Please hit me back as soon as you get this message."

After feeling her bottom one more time, making sure there were no wet spot showing, Jermonna opened the stall. Her cell phone was snatched out of her hand by the woman who Andrea had called Georgette. She quickly pushed Jermonna back into the stall, then locked the door, behind her.

"I don't think you'll be talking to Valerie Rollins or anyone else again in this lifetime!"

Before Jermonna could scream or try to push her off her, in one swift move, something sharp raked across her throat. Gasping for air, and unable to scream, Jermonna's last thought was, *what is my darling, Bartimaeus, going to do without me?*

Georgette took off the pink wig she was wearing and stuffed it in her purse. She made sure the bathroom was empty. She left the door locked and crawled under it, leaving Jermonna bleeding to death in the stall.

CHAPTER TWENTY-THREE

Danger and Heartbreak Dead Ahead

A FEW HOURS later

The décor of Valerie's office was as breathtaking as her library. To have a feeling of peace coupled with couture, all the furniture was white leather, including a sectional couch and four matching chairs. Her desk, file cabinets, table, floor lamps, and a chandelier, which were filled with white crystals. The only pop of color was her leopard print office chair, a rug, and pillows on the couch to match. There was a large abstract multi-colored flower painting covering one wall. The rest of the walls were filled with platinum records, including one from Michael Jackson, awards, plaques, and photos of Val's loved ones; her with countless celebrities, and her cousins. She was now recording the next day's radio feature.

"Hey, this is Gossip To Go With Valerie Ro. How's everyone doing on this Tasty Tuesday? According to page six of the New York Post, Kim Kardashian has filed for divorce from Kanye West after seven years of marriage. The couple had already been dealing with property settlements. Kim has filed for joint legal and physical custody of the couple's four children. This has been, Valerie Ro With Gossip To Go!"

Val felt relieved to finally finish her work for the day. After emailing the MP3 file, which she had recorded out to the twenty-five radio stations that carried her show. Valerie turned her ringer back on. Seeing Jermonna's number as a missed call, rather than listen to her message, she dialed her little buddy back. The call went straight to voicemail.

"Hey, J'Body. It is me, Val, returning your call. Holler at your girl."

After that tragic rollercoaster of a weekend, Val was holed up in her office all day making calls, writing a column and putting the radio show together. Cantrese had some loose ends needed to tie up in Los Angeles, so she was starting work in two weeks.

Rome was still dealing with searching through Dwayne's suite, as well as Amethyst's suicide attempt. With him seeing two murders right in front of him, coupled with Amethyst's breakdown, it caused Royale to have a severe migraine headache. He still suffered from the head injuries from when Rolondo knocked him out and his boat toppled over. The accident caused Royale to suffer from amnesia for five years. Val insisted he rested today. They could start turning the guest house into his team's headquarters tomorrow.

"Knock, knock."

A refreshed and revitalized Royale poked his head into her office.

Opening her arms to give her man a big hug, Val told him, "Come on in, baby. I'm just finishing up my work for the day. How are you feeling?"

Sitting on the edge of Valerie's desk and kissing her deeply, Royale said, "I feel much better. I am going to make an appointment with that neurologist you got me in New York in the next couple of weeks though."

"No problem. I will call his office for you tomorrow. It is going on six o'clock. I told Jonelle to do something tasty for dinner tonight like fried chicken. I can have her bring it up to our dining room. I think Esperanza and Kahari have already taken Valencia to McDonald's. I am not sure where Rome is."

"He's right here," said Rome, entering the office. "I am just getting back from Stony Brook Southampton Hospital. They are going to discharge Amethyst tomorrow morning. I don't know if I am doing the right thing, but I told her she could stay here with me for the time being."

"I think that is a good idea," said Val. "Is she getting some help?"

"Yes, she is getting help kicking the pills, which she had not taken in years, as well as her state of mind. I had no idea that she ever had an Opioid addiction, let alone that she was back on them. What are you two lovebirds up to?"

Before Val got a chance to answer Rome, her phone rang. She was not familiar with the number, which had a 313 area code, but she answered the call anyway.

"Hello."

There was a quivering man's voice on the other end.

"Hello, Ms. Valerie, this is Bartimaeus Sanford, Jermonna's fiancé."

"Hi, Bartimaeus. How are you? I just tried to call our girl, but her phone went straight to voicemail."

"Yes, I know it probably did. There is an awful reason why she is not answering her phone. I just received the most terrible news. Someone killed Jermonna. I just got a call from a security guard at Caesars Palace in Las Vegas, who is a fan of mine, and saw my number on Jermonna's phone. They found her in a locked stall in a bathroom with a slashed throat. I cannot begin to imagine what I am going to do without her, Ms. Valerie. Can you please meet me in Las Vegas by tomorrow morning? She still has you listed as her next of kin on all her important documents. I need your help."

"Are you sure she's dead?" Val whispered.

"I wish I wasn't sure, but my baby is gone," answered Bartimaeus. "The Las Vegas Medical Examiner's office has confirmed that she was murdered."

"All right. Rest assured that I will get out there as soon as possible. I am the executor of her estate. I will bring Jermonna's will with me. My family always stays at Caesars Palace. You are more than welcome to stay with us. I will also book a room for you. You best believe that I will find out who did this, okay? I will see you in Las Vegas tomorrow. Bye for now."

"Bye, Ms. Valerie," said Bartimaeus.

"Baby, what happened?" asked Royale, after Val hung up.

Barely able to talk, Val told him slowly, "Jermonna. Some animal slit her throat and left her to bleed out in a bathroom stall at Caesars Palace in Las Vegas. That was her fiancé on the phone."

Val started to moan loudly.

"I can't do this anymore. I cannot handle this daily dose of death that keeps engulfing my very soul. I feel like the grim reaper has taken over my life and will not leave me alone."

As Royale pulled her into his arms, Rome opened the mini-fridge in the office. He poured Valerie a glass of McBride Sisters' Chardonnay. She took a long sip of the soothing wine.

Rome asked Val, "I am so sorry. I know how much you love Jermonna. This all happened in Las Vegas, today?"

"Yes, that is what Bartimaeus just told me. Oh, no. Do you think whomever killed her may have been the same person threatening Dwayne about killing Valerian? Those text messages on Dwayne's phone are from a Las Vegas area code."

"It is a good possibility," said Rome. "We definitely should not rule the possible connection out."

Kahari knocked on the door.

"Excuse me, Ms. Val. Rome, Valerian is downstairs. He said you called him and told him it was important to meet with him over here right away."

"Yes, I did. Bring him to Valerie's office. I need to talk to him about the text messages on Dwayne's phone. Maybe he can shed some light on who Dwayne was talking to."

"Someone putting a hit on Sincere comes as no surprise to me. My cousin has been screwing over just about everyone he encounters since he was a teenager. Hell, if I could put a hit out on him, and get away with murder for hire, I would have done it years ago," said Royale.

"Is that so, Royale?" asked Valerian as he walked into Val's office. "And to think I always thought we were more like brothers than cousins."

"Have a seat, Valerian," said Valerie. "I was told your package was delivered earlier today."

"Yes, I got it. Thank you. So I am off your ass for the rest of the week. Now, what did you want to see me about, Rome? And Valerie, not that I really care, but why are there tears in your eyes?"

"I'll go first," said Rome. "While looking through Dwayne's phone for some clues as to who may have killed him, I found a thread of text messages between him and someone with a 702 area code. That person told Dwayne if he did not kill you, they were going to kill him. Somebody out there may have a hit out on you. Whomever it is, used a burner phone, so I was unable to trace the number."

For once, Valerian did not respond to Rome with his usual nasty retort.

Val spoke up.

"I just got a call from my best friend, Jermonna's, fiancé. He told me that she was killed this afternoon in Las Vegas. That is why I have been crying. Rome and I think that her murder may be connected to Dwayne's. I am listed as her next of kin, so I told Bartimaeus I will meet him in Vegas tomorrow morning."

"I knew Jermonna well," said Valerian. "When she was going through her addiction to drugs, and could not get any acting jobs, she worked for Rolondo and me in Vegas and throughout Europe, as an escort. Being a former television star was a big draw for wealthy men. I am sincerely sorry to hear that she is dead. I always liked her."

"Enough of your trip down pimp memory lane, Sincere," said Royale. "Can you think of anyone who would want to have Dwayne, Jermonna, and you killed?"

"No, cousin, I cannot. I have not traveled to, or done any business in Las Vegas for the last couple of years. Some of the Bugatti Blades are still using your Three Points Sports Bar as a meeting place though. But I do not have any beef with them."

"I have instructed my manager and staff to make sure no gang activity is going down at Three Points. I will have to speak to them about the Blades being on the premises."

"Just watch your back, Valerian. It looks like the guys, and I will be heading to Las Vegas tomorrow. Val, are you going to call Charmion over at Dumas Electronics to book the usual suites at Caesars Palace, while I tell the pilot and crew to get the large jet ready to leave. I am going to also lineup some additional security guys for us out there since it looks like there is a murderer on the loose," Rome said.

"Yes, I'll call her right away. I think I will ask her to work with me in Las Vegas this week. Royale, can you come with us? I know you want to start getting your office together."

"Baby, I am not ever leaving your side again. There is nothing that can stop me from going with you. While I am in

Las Vegas, I can also pay my sports bar a visit to get things in order there."

"If you don't mind," said Valerian. "I would like to come with you too. Since my life may be on the line, I will call a meeting of the Sin City Bugatti Blades to see what they know."

"It is cool with me if Val says it's okay," said Rome. "Maybe your being with us will lure the killer out of his cocoon."

Val only had energy to nod her head *yes*.

Looking at a text message, Rome told Valerian, "We will pick you up at the American Hotel in the morning at eight, then head to Kennedy Airport. This is odd. I just received an alert that the jet Vance flew to Texas in yesterday, just landed in Las Vegas. I wonder what made him decide to head out there without telling us."

"I don't know," said Valerie. "I haven't been able to get in touch with him since we had brunch with him."

Said Valerian, "Some little birdie informed me earlier today that Vance and Johnyce could be getting ready to go on a honeymoon."

Val, Rome, and Royale all simultaneously yelled, "What!"

"Who do you know that is privy to anything Vance got going on, cousin?" asked Royale.

"Since we are taking this short hiatus from me pouring misery down all three of your throats, I will admit that Ashro and the Knox twins work for me. I sicced them on Vance in Las Vegas. Even though I only have thoroughbred hoes in my stable that specialize in knowing how to keep a man's dick hard, I had no idea he would be so foolish as to move the bitches in his house. I just wanted them to milk a few million dollars out of him, then give a huge portion of it to me, which was easily carried out. Anyway, Vance called Ashro last night to tell her the party is over because he and Pastor Johnyce are in love with each other. As you know, she is one of Claude's girls, so she also has a degree in pussy whipping a man. Anyway, Ashro, Sapphire, and Saffron flew back to Las Vegas this afternoon."

"I should kick your ass for setting up Vance like that, Sincere," said Royale. "Do you have any shame? Vance is the father of your granddaughter. Why would you do something like that to him?"

"You know that I have always loved money over family, cousin."

"I agree with Royale. Your viciousness runs way too deep, Valerian. But can somebody tell me whether I did something terrible in a past life? My best friend, who is like my baby sister, has been murdered, and now my bonus son has fallen in love at first sight with a preacher who doubles as a prostitute, who he only met two days ago. Father God, I need anointing," Valerie said.

"No, Vance needs anointing, or spiritual cleansing, and so do you, Sincere. Let me see if he will pick up for me," said Royale before shouting into his phone. "Call Vance."

"Hey, cousin," said Vance. "I was just getting ready to call Valerie. For some reason, she has been blowing up my phone today. What's up?"

"Valerie is right here. I am putting you on speaker so Rome can also hear this conversation. Sincere is here with us too, and he just informed us that you and Johnyce have fallen in love and in Las Vegas. For once, I sure hope my cousin is lying, as usual," Royale told him.

"How the hell did Valerian find out? I did not want you all to hear about my marriage this way," said Vance.

"Your marriage!" shouted Val.

"You should not talk about me like I'm not here, Vance," said Sincere. "Your former live in pussy posse works for me. They told me all about it before they hightailed it out of the Hamptons. You better hope you have any valuables left in that fuck tank of a mansion you live in. I would bet those three thieves snatched up everything they could pack into their Louis Vuitton luggage."

"Vance, how did you come to this decision?" asked Valerie. "This is real life, not a movie or a dress rehearsal. Johnyce seems like a lovely young woman, but this is too fast. Have you even thought of getting a prenuptial agreement?"

"Yes, Val. I had my lawyer draw up one and email it to me while we were flying out here. Johnyce signed it right away with no hesitation. We fell in love, Val. We are getting married tomorrow whether you like it or not. She also wants Valencia to come live with us. No other woman that I have been involved with has ever told me that. My baby girl's own mother did not even want her. Johnyce is a rare jewel."

"Well, we are all coming out there tomorrow. Jermonna was killed, and I have to identify her body and take care of the arrangements. Can you at least wait to have the wedding until we get there, so we can be with you? I do not want to bring Valencia with me though because it looks like the same person that may have killed Dwayne and Jermonna could be right there in Las Vegas. It is best to leave her here with extra security," said Valerie.

"I heard about Jermonna's murder. I am very sorry, Val. It is all anyone is talking about in this entire town. I know how close you two were. Yes, Johnyce and I can hold the wedding tomorrow night. I will text you the details. Are you planning to stay at Caesars Palace? We are here in the Palace Manor Villa in Palace Tower."

"Yes, we are going to check into Caesars as we always do. I am going to have Charmion take care of the reservations as soon as I finish talking to you. I also have some particularly important business to discuss with you, which is why I have been trying to reach you."

"What is it?" asked Vance. "We are all amongst family, even though I hate that Valerian is related to us."

"It actually concerns Valerian," said Val. "I have offered your uncle two billion dollars to sign an agreement to stop harassing us. I gave him a ten million dollars advance this morning. Are you all right with my decision?"

"Hell yes," said Vance. "We can always make more money to replace it. If that is what it takes to get you out of our lives, Uncle Valerian, help yourself to the cash. Good riddance. Is that all, Val? I was about to head out to pick up Johnyce from Brilliant Bridal over on Sahara where she is buying a wedding gown and shoes. Then we have an appointment at T-Bird Jewels to pick out rings."

"That is all I have to say for now. We will see you tomorrow morning in Las Vegas."

"Do not hang up yet, Vance," said Royale. "I have something to ask you and Valerie."

"What is it, cousin?" asked Vance.

"Can we make it a double wedding tomorrow night? You might as well get your money's worth. Is that okay with you, Val?"

"Yes, it is, Royale. It will bring some sunshine into these dark nightmarish three days of tragedies we have been going through. I cannot bring back Dwayne or Jermonna, but I always wanted my life to be a romantic comedy with a happy ending. Let the sadness stop here."

"I'm down with it too," said Vance. "I will see you all tomorrow. Bye for now."

Val turned her attention to Valerian.

"We have Vance's blessing, but I will never trust you. By Friday, you have to give me your answer."

"Whatever. All this love swirling around me is making me sick to my stomach. I am out of here. I will be in front of the hotel in the morning. I must say, I will be happy to get out of the Hamptons and especially away from you, Royale. I do not want your nice guy personae to rub off on me, cousin."

With those words, Valerian left Val's office.

Rome smiled at Val.

"I think your charm is turning Valerian into a human being, Val. Let's go down to the dining room to eat. Then I will head to my office to get everything ready for our trip. How long do you think we are going to have to stay in Vegas?"

"At least until the weekend. Since I am the executor of Jermonna's estate, if it is okay with Bartimaeus, I want to bring her body back here, and bury her on the property. I can create a beautiful resting place for her on that land past the stables on the water. Once we find out if Dwayne has any family, if they like, we can also bury him there. If we can't locate any relatives of his, I planned for Benta Funeral Home in Harlem to pick up his remains, then prepare his body. We will have services for both Dwayne and Jermonna next week."

Val started crying again.

"Come on, baby," said Royale. "Rome is right. It is time for you to get something to eat. You have been working all day, and the rest of the week is going to be rough."

Unfortunately, Royale had no idea *rough* could not begin to describe what was about to transpire for all of them over the next few days.

CHAPTER TWENTY-FOUR

Evil Hijacks A Wedding Eve

Following spending a half-million dollars on huge diamond wedding bands by Christopher Designs, Vance took Johnyce shopping for wedding wardrobe at Saks Fifth Avenue. After buying a dozen new outfits, which included couture dresses, pants sets, and lingerie from Yves Saint Laurent, Givenchy, Burberry, Versace, and a few other designers, they were now in the shoe department, where his fiancé tried on Christian Louboutin shoes to match each piece of clothing. Johnyce had fallen so in love with one of the Versace garments that she had changed into it.

A woman wearing a crazy looking pink wig with a matching face mask was also trying on the costly Red Bottom shoes. When her eyes met Vance's, she looked as if she had stumbled upon a ghost.

Thinking she must be a fan, Vance greeted her.

"Hello, ma'am. I am Vance Dumas. Have you been to any of my horse races?"

Gaining her composure, the woman said, "I thought that was you, Mr. Dumas. My name is Gigi. I am a huge fan of yours. I even know, I mean, I knew your mother, Andrea. We used to model together before you were born. It is so nice to meet you."

Georgette thought to herself, *I'm grateful I cleaned that up and didn't let Andrea's present status of being among the living be known.*

"It is so nice to meet you too. I have never met any of my mother's friends other than my Uncle Valerian and his cousin, Royale Jones. This is my fiancé, Johnyce Parks. We are getting married tomorrow at the Venus Garden Chapel at Caesars Palace at seven p.m. Since you were a friend of my mom's, I would love it if you could attend."

Johnyce extended her hand to Gigi.

"It is genuinely nice to meet you, ma'am. I love your pink hair. It is the new rage. My favorite tennis player, Naomi Osaka, dyed her hair pink after she won the Australian Open. That would be so nice for Vance to have a friend of his mother's at our wedding. I am excited that it is also going to be a double wedding. Vance's stepmother and his cousin are also getting married. They have been in love for almost forty years, but just got back together. I think that is so romantic."

Georgette could not believe the information she had stumbled upon. These nuggets were the Rolls Royce of pay dirt. She knew Aurora was going to lay some heavy bread on her for this newfound knowledge.

"I would love to be there. I think I read somewhere that your father, Victor Dumas, married Valerie Rollins, the gossip columnist, right? And then he sadly passed away from cancer."

"Yes, that is true. She is marrying my cousin, Royale Jones, who is a retired baseball player. As my fiancé just told you, they were college sweethearts."

Gigi pulled out her phone.

Scrolling through her photos, she told Vance, "I am pretty sure I have a picture on here of Andrea and me modeling for Grace Del Marco, the first Black modeling agency owned by Ophelia DeVore, at the Cannes Film Festival back in the 1970s."

"Bingo! I found it," she told Vance as she handed him the phone.

"Wow," said Vance. "You two were something else. Very beautiful!"

As Johnyce told the shoe salesman which styles she was buying, Vance made Gigi an offer.

"Let me pay for whatever Red Bottoms you want to buy. I feel like I have met my long-lost aunt. Then, please join us for cocktails and a bite to eat at The Palm."

"I cannot let you do that," said Georgette. "These two pairs of shoes come to at least sixteen hundred dollars."

"Yes, you can."

He then told the salesperson, "Please ring these two pairs up with my fiancé's shoes, then put them in a separate bag for Ms. Gigi."

Taking a pair of Versace Medusa Chain Patent Leather Platform Mules out of a box, and putting the shoes she was wearing in it, Johnyce told the salesperson, "I'm going to wear these out. They go perfectly with my new dress. I just love them!"

"You are too kind. Your personality is just like your mother's. Do you mind if I make a mad dash into the ladies' room before we head over to the The Palm? I would be honored to join you two lovebirds for a cocktail," Gigi told Vance.

"Go ahead now," said Johnyce. "Vance and I will wait right here for you while our new shoes are being wrapped up."

"Thank you," said Georgette. "I'll be fast."

Georgette practically ran to the bathroom, which fortunately was found on the same floor as the shoe department. Georgette pulled out her phone to call Aurora once she entered a stall.

"Yes," said Aurora, who picked up on the first ring.

"Girl, I hope you are sitting down. I just ran into your son and his fiancé in the shoe department in Saks. I told him we were friends when you were alive and showed him a picture of us on the runway at Cannes back in the day. Not only did he buy me two pairs of Red Bottoms, but then he invited me to join them for cocktails and din din at The Palm over in the Forum Shops at Caesars. Her name is Johnyce. What do you want me to do?"

"I knew there was a reason we have been best friends for most of our sixty years on this earth. You are always in the right place at the right time. This is fate. It is payback time for Vance Dumas. He just went ahead like business as usual when he thought I was killed. On top of that, he married my little piece, Roshonda. The little bastard never even mourned for me; the woman who brought him into this world. Forget going to The Palm. Tell Vance that it would be more convenient for you to have a drink with them right there in the mall at The Capital Grille. He always liked the food there. I love the fact that I have an opportunity to get my hands on those Dumas' billions so fast. Does he have any security with him?"

"Yes, just one guy," answered Georgette. "He will not be a problem."

"During dinner, tell them you would like to treat them to a wedding drink at the Three Points Sports Bar, which was my favorite hangout in Las Vegas. I will be there when you all arrive with some Bugatti Blades, who will hijack their car the moment you drive up. Although I checked into the Wynn Hotel, I just got the keys to the house I had Jamal rent for me out in the desert. The guys can bring Vance and his bride here. You got all this? If that little polo playing punk wants to get married tomorrow, he will get money wired into the account number I am going to give him right away. I will keep my face mask on, so he will never know it is me, or that you had them snatched. I still want to have Sincere killed, and get even with Valerie Rollins. But in this life, I have learned you cannot have it all."

"You may have a chance to get even with Valerie tomorrow. Vance and Johnyce are having a double wedding with her and Royale Jones."

"Really? I grew up with him. He is Sincere's cousin. It looks like everyone will find out the true meaning of a shotgun wedding tomorrow. This should be a blast! See you later. I will have some additional bread to lay on you."

Gigi hurried back to where Vance was giving the salesperson information to have all Johnyce's purchases delivered to Caesars Palace. He handed Gigi the shopping bags, which held her new shoes.

"I do not how to thank you, Vance. This is a wonderful treat."

"You are very welcome. I assume that you are driving. Do you want to meet us over at The Palm?"

"I actually have a better idea. Why don't we have dinner right here in the Fashion Show Mall at The Grille? Then I would like to do something special for you to thank you for the shoes. I will treat you almost newlyweds to after-dinner drinks at your mother's favorite place in town, The Three Points Sports Bar & Grill."

"I know the Three Points was my mom's favorite spot here. That is where they found her dead. I have always wanted to see the last place my mother was alive. It will be my pleasure to go there with you. I will finally get some closure on my mother's murder. I also happen to like The Capital Grille. My dad and I used to eat there all the time when we were here in Vegas together. Come on, Johnyce. We have a fun wedding night eve ahead of us!" said Vance.

"In your wildest dreams, you have never had as much fun as tonight is going to be," said Georgette.

CHAPTER TWENTY-FIVE

The Bachelor/Bachelorette Bash
Ends With a Bang

SINCE HE WAS A KID, and his father used to bring him to Las Vegas with him, Vance had loved eating at The Capital Grille. He enjoyed the acclaimed dry aged steaks, world-class wines, and the spectacular view at this restaurant. Their meal was now winding down.

Finishing her food, Johnyce told Vance and Gigi, "I have never tasted food this good before. I hope I can still fit into my wedding gown tomorrow."

Gigi took the final bite of her tenderloin and lobster, washing it down with a Capital Cosmopolitan, which she had four too many of. "Your mother just told me this was always your favorite restaurant," she blurted.

Smiling at her, Vance said, "This is the second time this afternoon that you referred to my mom in the present tense, Ms. Gigi. I think we had better forget going to Three Points Sports Bar and call an Uber to get you wherever you need to go. The drinks seem to have gotten to you."

Georgette was tired of the charade she was putting on. To be so young, Vance and his bride-to-be were too lovey dovey for her to spend another moment with them. She was also having second thoughts about taking part in Andrea's plans to kidnap them. Like Dwayne, she was too old to go to prison. Whether she was drunk, high, or sober she was going to get in her car and head home to Los Angeles.

"You caught me," said Gigi. "I am also a little high. I did a little blow when I went to the little girl's room earlier. Your mother and me, and her friend Betty, have always loved to get high. You look like a chick who may like to indulge Johnyce. You want to take a little walk with me?"

"No thank you, ma'am. I will stick with the champagne."

"My mother and her addiction to drugs usage caused a lot of pain in my childhood," said Vance.

"She would run off with her friends and leave Dad and me alone on the ranch sometimes for months. Many times, while she was under the influence, she would beat me. So, I would rather you not talk about that side of her, Ms. Gigi, if you do not mind. We have had such a lovely time together so far."

Georgette stood up, then grabbed the shopping bag.

"You know, the things that Andrea always says about you are true. You are nothing but a spoiled, little polo playing brat. Thanks for the Louboutins. I am out of here! Nice meeting you. Good luck because if your mom gets her way, you may not make it to the altar tomorrow!"

"My mother is dead, lady!" Vance yelled, as Gigi stomped away from the booth.

"What just happened? She seemed so nice at first," remarked Johnyce.

"I'm not surprised a friend of my mother's went all postal

on us so quickly. You can bet if she hung around my mom and Violet's mother, Betty, she was just a drug addicted slut like they were. I should not have gotten so excited when we met her at Saks. But for a minute, being around Gigi was like having my mom with me when she felt like being nice."

"It is going to be all right, baby. She really sounded crazy, referring to your mom as if she is alive."

"Forget what just happened. We are celebrating our love! Waiter, bring my fiancé another bottle of Moet Rose' Imperial Brut Champagne!"

* * *

Wearing a Vivica A. Fox, curly black wig, and huge sunglasses under a wide brimmed black hat, Aurora watched Vance and Johnyce from the other side of the restaurant, indulging in a long kiss.

Something had told her Georgette was going to fuck up her instructions. So, just in case, she had made alternate plans. Listening to the way Vance talked about her, calling her an abusive mother, let her know she was doing the right thing. Forgetting to ask the server for her check, Aurora put on her sequin face mask and headed to the door to catch up with Georgette. It was time to get rid of her.

"Miss, I need to give you your check!" yelled the waiter, running after her with the bill in his hand.

"I am sorry. I forgot all about it."

To retrieve her wallet, Aurora had to take off her sunglasses so she could look in the bottom of her Hermès Birkin bag, where it was buried. Forgetting to put the shades back on, Aurora turned around, flinging a fifty-dollar bill at the young man. For an instant, Vance's distinctively green eyes looked straight into her eyes, which were identical to his. Putting the glasses back on quickly, Aurora made a fast exit from the restaurant.

Looking around for Georgette, Aurora spotted her, slightly staggering out of the bathroom. She walked swiftly up to her, grabbed her arm, then practically dragged Georgette to the nearest exit. She didn't stop until they were outside in the parking lot.

"What are you thinking, getting drunk and high, then practically shouting to the world that I am still alive?" Aurora asked Georgette.

Snatching her arm away, Georgette answered, "Oh, who cares? There was a time when you got high before drinking your morning coffee, so do not judge me. Plus, I am positive that Vance did not pay my unintended blunders any attention. Please don't hurt me, but I'm not feeling well. I am heading back to Los Angeles, Andrea. It was good seeing you. Let's get together again real soon."

Andrea leaned in close to Georgette. "My name is Aurora. You know we have been hanging out at bars until they closed for many years. Girlfriend, this is your last call for a deadly diva," Andrea whispered in her ear before plunging a syringe filled with pure heroin laced and rat poison through Georgette's dress, directly into her heart.

As Georgette slumped to the ground, Aurora yelled, "Help! Help! Something just happened to my friend." She hopped into a black-on-black Nissan Rogue with dark tinted windows, and sped off.

Kwami tailed Vance and Johnyce closely as they approached the parking lot to get into the chauffeured Bentley Bentayga Vance had hired to transport them around during their stay in Las Vegas. Johnyce noticed a small crowd gathering around a woman on the ground. Her feet were visible. Johnyce recognized the multi-colored Christian Louboutin sneakers that the eccentric woman was wearing, as well as the shopping bag she carried on the ground next to her.

"Vance," she said. "That is Gigi. Something happened to her!"

Before Johnyce could run over to see what happened, she noticed the driver got out of the Bentley as soon as he drove up, then walked away swiftly. The security person who had been with him was not in the front seat either. Being on the streets most of her life had taught Johnyce to be naturally suspicious of unusual activity. There was something strange going on. Suddenly, she saw sparks shooting from beneath the car. Before Kwami could open the door for them, Johnyce yelled.

"There may be a bomb under the car! Kwami, get away from the car!" She grabbed Vance's hand. She ran as fast as her legs could carry her in five-inch heels back toward the entrance to the mall. The last thing she heard was a loud bang as Kwami pushed her and Vance onto the concrete. The world around Johnyce faded to black.

CHAPTER TWENTY-SIX

Only The Strong Survive

As the Bentley became engulfed in flames, Vance heard Kwami's voice.

"Vance, Johnyce, are you all right?" asked Kwami as he slowly climbed off them, helping Vance up.

"Yeah, man, I'm cool."

When Vance stood up, he saw that Johnyce's eyes were closed and she was laying very still.

He kneeled back down and picked her up.

"Baby, please talk to me."

Johnyce slowly opened her eyes.

"Vance, honey, I thought I was going to lose you. But you are still with me."

As he helped her stand up, Vance told Johnyce, "I am always going to be with you. We are together for life. Your fast reaction saved our lives. We would have been history if you would not have stopped us from getting in the car before grabbing my hand and running. What caused you to do that?"

"I saw the driver get out and move away from the car quickly, and the security guard wasn't in the car either. Then I saw sparks shoot out."

Vance held Johnyce tightly in his arms.

"I told you that you are an angel sent to me from God. I love you, baby."

A flurry of sirens filled the air as fire trucks pulled up and firemen jumped out, unraveling hoses to put out the fire.

Two police officers and paramedics with stretchers approached them.

"Please move back," said one officer, who looked at Vance. "Aren't you Vance Dumas, the jockey?"

"Yes, sir, I am."

"I thought so. I am a huge fan. A gentleman standing over there told us you were about to get into the car right before it exploded. Is that true?"

"Yes, it is. My fiancé noticed the driver get out of the car, then abandon it. Then she saw sparks coming from under it. That made her grab my hand and run. Her fast thinking is the only reason we are still alive."

"Do you know of anyone who would want to harm you?" asked the officer.

"Not really. My Uncle Valerian Davidson is always threatening me, but he wants money. If I die, he can't get any cash out of me, so I don't think he had the explosives planted under the car, which is rented. I had the hotel get the driver for me, and the head of Dumas Electronics, Rome Nyland, hired the extra security person for me. I will check with him."

"Rome's phone went straight to voicemail. I left him a message about what happened. I am going to call an Uber to get us back to the hotel," said Kwami.

"All right," said Vance. "Officer, if you have any more questions, I can be reached at Caesars Palace."

"Officer?" asked Johnyce. "When we came out here, there was a woman lying there. I see the ambulance must have taken her away. Do you know what happened to her?"

"She was pronounced dead. The medical examiner took her body to the morgue. We do not know who she really was because she had four different driver's licenses in her wallet. They all had her picture on them. Why do you ask?"

Since someone had attempted to kill them after having lunch with the mysterious Gigi, Johnyce's street sense told her it was best not to tell the police anything that could put her and Vance in more danger.

"I was just curious," answered Johnyce, as a black Lincoln Town car pulled up in front of them.

"Come on, Vance and Johnyce, this is our Uber," said Kwami. "I want to get you two back to the safety of the hotel as fast as possible."

As they entered the vehicle, they didn't notice the black-on-black Nissan Rogue idling a few car lengths ahead of them.

CHAPTER TWENTY-SEVEN

When The Fairy Tale Comes to Fruition

IT WAS ALMOST eleven at night back on the east coast. With no time to go shopping, Valerie was in her closet, trying to put a wedding trousseau together, as well as finding proper attire to mourn Jermonna in. Many people only went to church for weddings and funerals. Never in her wildest dreams did she imagine she would have to deal with both happy and sad occasions at one time.

Victor's decorator had Valerie's closet built on to the master bedroom suite. White walls with white plush carpet, the luxurious closet was the size of four large bedrooms, with a large chandelier hanging in the middle of all the customized clothes cubicles, drawers for four-hundred pairs of shoes, countless purses, sweaters, lingerie, and coats. A large silver ottoman sat in the middle of everything, and there was an eighty-inch television screen on the wall. Val selected an off the shoulder silver sequin gown, along with a pair of Valentino Atelier Floral leather slide sandals to get married in. While placing the items in her suitcase, she heard the newscaster on ABC Eyewitness News. *"Breaking News! Popular jockey, Vance Dumas, his fiancé, Johnyce Parks, and their bodyguard, Kwami Reynolds, had a brush with death in Las Vegas earlier this evening when their rented Bentley Bentayga exploded in the valet parking lot of the Fashion Showcase Mall. Vance told authorities that Johnyce's quick thinking saved their lives. Ladies, I guess this means that the billionaire bachelor is off the market. Stay tuned to learn more about the mysterious Miss Johnyce Parks! Whoever she is, she is one lucky woman!"*

Val stopped packing and ran downstairs to the den where Rome and Royale were going over the coordination for tomorrow's trip. Rome was on his phone.

"I just saw on the news that Vance, Kwami, and Johnyce were almost killed earlier today when the car he rented exploded!" Val exclaimed.

"We know, baby," said Royale. "Rome is talking to him now. Vance just got a chance to call him because Johnyce's head started to hurt badly, so they took her to the hospital to get examined."

Rome nodded at Val.

"Vance, Val just walked into the den. I want to bring her up to speed. We are landing in Las Vegas tomorrow morning at eleven. I will switch security companies right away and have the new one post some more guys outside of your suite. Until we get there, I do not want you, Johnyce, or Kwami to step one foot outside of there. Do you understand me?"

"Yes, I do. Can I speak to Royale real fast?"

"Okay."

Rome handed the phone to Royale.

"Vance wants to speak to you."

"Hey, little cuz. Thank God you are okay."

"Thanks to Johnyce. She really does have a special connection with God. I have a question to ask you. Will you be my best man tomorrow? And, let Val know that Johnyce would like her to be her Maid of Honor."

"I would be very honored to be your Best Man, but only if you will do the same thing for me."

"You got it! We will see you tomorrow. I am going to get some rest. This has been one explosive day, no pun intended."

"Goodnight. Stay safe, Vance. We all love you!"

"Rome, does Vance have any idea who could have put a bomb under that car?" asked Val.

"No, he does not. However, he told me he ran into a woman named Gigi in Saks Fifth Avenue who told him she had been best friends with his mother. She even showed him a photo of her and Andrea from their modeling days that she had on her phone. He was so excited to see the photo of Andrea that he paid for her purchases. Then invited her to join him and Johnyce for dinner, where she became drunk and started talking about Andrea as if she is alive. Then she left in a huff. When he and Johnyce were outside of the mall, the woman was lying on the ground. The police later told Vance she was dead."

"I know exactly who Gigi is," said Royale. "She and Andrea were thicker than thieves when they were in their twenties. I do not know if she still lives in Las Vegas, but she used to. Her real name is Georgette Walters. She could be who Dwayne was texting back and forth because she used to hang out in my bar with Sincere while I was playing with the Los Angeles Wildcats. I remember she was so in love with him, but he was more into Andrea. Anyway, he accidentally shot this Gigi one night. She survived the incident physically, but suffered a mental breakdown and was never the same. She confronted him one night, and told Sincere that one day, when he least expected it, she was going to get even and kill him."

"So, if she knew Valerian, and Jermonna also worked for

him, maybe she ran into her at Caesars Palace, and they had some sort of disagreement, and she killed her. The hotel security has footage of Jermonna talking with two women who were in the bar. When we get there tomorrow they are going to show it to me," said Val. "They have already given the police a copy of the videotape. But the questions are, how did this Gigi die? And did she have something to do with the bomb underneath the car?"

"Val," said Royale. "Right now, we can trust very few people. Since I have hired Rafael to work with me, I spoke to his parole officer and asked if he could accompany us to Las Vegas tomorrow. He is very streetwise, and some of the guys he was in prison with have their ears to the streets out there in Vegas. His parole officer emailed me the proper documents for him to accompany us. I had an Uber pick him up at the A-loft Hotel in Harlem. He should be here soon."

"Lastly," said Rome. "Since I am paying for her treatment, the rehabilitation center is going to keep Amethyst there until we get back. So, she will be taken care of."

"Val," said Royale. "Vance told me that Johnyce would like you to be her Maid of Honor."

"Since there doesn't seem to be anything I can do to stop this live family version of 'Married at First Sight,' it would be my pleasure. All right. It seems as if everything is in order, so I am going to finish packing. I will see you at seven in the morning, Rome. Are you coming upstairs, Royale?"

"Yes, but first I want to give you a little something something."

He then hit a button on the in-house phone. Even though he only lived with Val for two days, Royale had familiarized himself with the technology around her home.

"Jonelle, you can bring the champagne to the den now. Thank you."

"I was waiting for you to finish your packing, but since you are already down here, we may as well do this now," he told Val.

"Do what?" asked Val.

Jonelle and two of the maids entered the den with a rolling cart filled with several bottles of champagne, glasses, a platter of shrimp cocktails, caviars, and crackers.

Rafael entered the den right behind them.

"I see I am just in time for the wedding eve party."

"Yes, you are, cousin. Have a seat."

Jonelle filled four flutes with champagne while the maids served them.

Valerie watched in awe as Royale got down on one knee, removed the ring she was wearing off her finger, then replaced it with the biggest diamond ring she had ever laid eyes on.

"Tomorrow, we will finally become husband and wife. Welcome to the fairy tale, baby!"

CHAPTER TWENTY-EIGHT

Aurora and Jamal
Raging Revenge

Unbeknownst to Vance, Jamal had gone with Sapphire, Saffron, and Ashro to Las Vegas, and the four of them hooked up with Aurora. The polo player was behind the wheel of the Nissan Rogue, with Sapphire sitting next to him. Saffron and Ashro sat in the back seat alongside Aurora.

"Jamal, hon. I don't know if I think it was such a good idea for you to fly out here. Vance is no dummy. We have kept our intimate relationship a secret since you two were eighteen. Until I get my hands on that Dumas' fortune, we do not need him to figure things out since he is still alive," said Aurora.

"I could care less what that spoiled brat finds out," said Jamal. "I have never understood why we had to keep our affair a secret anyway."

"Duh, because if Victor ever found out, he would have found a way to divorce me as well as throw your young ass right off the farm," explained Aurora. "I can't believe Vance changed his mind and didn't get into that Bentley after we paid the valet parking attendant to take a break so I could toss that stick of dynamite underneath the car. I've been trying to get rid of him since before he was born. His father stormed into the clinic and halted the abortion I was about to have. I even tried to drown him in the bathtub. Then the nanny came in and saved him. That boy has nine lives."

"So?" asked Jamal. "What is your next move? Vance called everyone on the polo team to let us know he is getting married tomorrow. Of course, Sapphire had already told me. On the phone calls, Vance said he will be back in the Hamptons on Friday to resume practice, then take his bride, whomever she is, on a honeymoon after our next polo match. I told Nino and Lee that I had an emergency out of town, so I would be missing practice for a few days. The Dumas Diamonds Polo Club plays in Monte Carlo next month, and no matter what happens, I want to be with the team. It has always been my dream to play in Monaco."

"You and Vance and those damn horses. You are more alike than you think. Since you are here, you may as well make yourself useful. Call Vance and tell him that you have some unexpected business in town that is an emergency, but since you are here, you would love to attend his wedding tomorrow. After all, you two did grow up together. Then, some of the Bugatti Blades that work at Caesars Palace and I will show up for the nuptials. I will take it from there. No one will ever have to know anything about our past personal business."

Jamal was beginning to regret when Andrea had called him with her sordid plan. He flew with his woman, her sister, and friend. Although it would be nice to be rid of Vance, and steal his money, what if they couldn't get away with killing the bastard? Rome was pretty smart. He could smell danger miles away.

"Drop me off at the Wynn, baby," said Aurora. "It's right across the street. I am going to call it a night. I will see you and your lady friends tomorrow."

"You can also drop us off here," said Sapphire. "I have a date with a long-time regular that is going to lay some heavy bread on the three of us. Call me tomorrow. I am also going to see if Vance wants a *goodbye to being a bachelor* blow job tonight."

"I can't believe this is the first time in a while that we have a chance to spend the entire night together without sneaking around, and you pick some John and Vance over me," said Jamal.

She got out of the car and kissed him on the cheek. "You may be cute, baby, but your money will never be long enough for me. You cannot afford to keep me in Red Bottoms or new Birkins. Like I said, I will speak to you tomorrow," Sapphire told him.

"What you just said is not true, Sapphire. You have a very selective memory. I have bought you two pairs of Red Bottoms and a Chanel bag," said Jamal.

"Whatever. Now, if you want to call me tomorrow, be my guest. I am finished talking for now. We have to bounce," said Sapphire, as the parking valet attendant in front of the Wynn Hotel helped her out of the SUV.

Jamal pulled up a few feet, took out his cell phone, then punched up Vance.

"Hey, man," said Vance. "I just hung up with Nino, and he told me you flew out of town to handle some important business. Is everything okay?"

"Yeah, I'm cool. I had to head out here to Las Vegas for an important meeting with my agent and some people about a new endorsement deal that couldn't wait."

"You don't have to lie to me. I am sure your ass is out here chasing Sapphire. I know she has your nose wide open. She was living with me, and you are staying on my horse training facility, so you have to be crazy to even imagine you could keep your fling with her a secret from me," said Vance.

"Damn, man. Is it a problem?"

"Only when it interferes with my polo team, like it seems to be doing. But since you are in town, you might as well come to my wedding tomorrow, then get your ass on a plane back to the Hamptons on Thursday. Are you staying with Sapphire?"

"I am sorry, man. You know me. I would never do anything behind your back, but I got caught up in the web of a very fine and seductive woman. But, to answer your question, I am not staying with her. She just told me she has plans for the night. I am in front of the Wynn Hotel, so I will see if they have a room that I can check into for two nights," Jamal told Vance.

"You don't have to do that," said Vance. "Come on over to Caesars Palace. I am in one of the villas. You can stay here with us. There is plenty of room. I can use a childhood friend over here. Someone tried to blow up the car I rented today. My fiancé saved both of our lives, as well as Kwami's. We will talk when you get here. I will have Kwami notify the front desk that you are on the way."

"Thanks, man. I cannot wait to meet this *instant* fiancé of yours."

"I bet you can't. Just so you know, if you even try to hit on her like you did Sapphire, or all of those chicks I was boning when we were kids, your ass is grass," laughed Vance.

As Jamal disconnected the call, he said to himself, "My ass will be just fine, you spoiled son of a bitch. But tomorrow, if your mother has her way, your ass may be finished."

CHAPTER TWENTY-NINE

Wednesday Hump Day in The Friendly Skies

STILL IN SHOCK from Jermonna being murdered in cold blood, and that after all these years she was about to fulfill her dream of becoming Mrs. Royale Jones, Valerie had spent the entire five hour flight to Las Vegas in her jet's bedroom, with Royale's arms wrapped, around her. She was simply too weary to sit up.

One of her flight attendants, Sandra, knocked lightly on the door.

"Yes?" asked Val.

"We are going to be landing in about an hour, Ms. Valerie. Do you need anything?"

"No, I'm fine. We will be right out. Thank you."

"How are you doing, baby?" asked Royale.

"Not great, but I have to keep going."

"Once we get past our wedding tonight, and you have services for Jermonna and Dwayne, you are putting aside this need to 'have to keep going' and taking a break. If you agree to it, I am going to lease a yacht for us when we go to the South of

France for the Dumas Diamonds Polo Club's tournament. When we leave Monaco, I want to sail around the South of France for the rest of the summer, just you and me."

"That would be lovely. I am in total agreement. Although I feel like time stood still for us, it will also give us a chance to really get to know each other again. I love you, Mr. Jones."

"I love you more, Ms. Rollins."

Val stood up.

Taking Royale's hand in hers, she opened the door to the main cabin.

"Come on. For now, we still live in the real world."

"Well. . . well. . . well. . . the almost Mr. and Mrs. Jones have decided to grace us with their presence," said Valerian.

Looking around the jet's cabin lined with rich cream leather seats and custom wood veneer, with fur-like carpet and shining stonework. In addition to the bedroom, the jet included a full dining room, and bathroom.

"Throw in this jet, Valerie, and we have a deal. Hell, if I can own this baby, I may even give you and Royale a wedding gift," Valerian, the con man, continued.

"We don't need or want any present from you, Sincere," quipped Royale as he helped Valerie into a seat.

"Valerian, I will happily give you this jet if that is what it takes to keep you from continuously trying to harm us. I prefer traveling in one of the smaller ones anyway. Can we at least go back home in this jet though, or do we all need to catch a ride back with Vance and Johnyce?" asked Val.

"No, you can go back home the way you came here, but I want the deed to this fine aircraft and the money in my bank account by Monday."

"Your wish is my command," said Val sarcastically.

"Val," said Rome. "Rafael, Valerian, and I have been doing some research on this woman, Georgette, while you were resting. Take a look at these photos that hotel security emailed me of the women Jermonna was talking to in the bar. Valerian says this one is definitely Georgette. However, the other woman must know the bar area in Caesars well because she never showed her face to the camera. You can only see the rhinestones on the rim that goes around her ears on the sunglasses that she is wearing. Georgette followed Jermonna to the bathroom, and even though she changed wigs while she was in there, the authorities are positive she is the murderer. But as Vance told us last night, she is now dead. So, my theory is whoever killed her is most likely the mastermind behind Dwayne's murder, the attempt on Vance's life, and a possible hit out on Valerian."

"All right. As soon as we check into the hotel and drop the luggage off, I need to identify Jermonna's body. I have already arranged for Lake Memorials Celebrations of Life to pick her up. After that, can we go to Royale's bar and show his staff these photos to see what they know? From there, I would like you to run an errand with me, Rafael. After that, it will be time to get ready for tonight's weddings. Does that itinerary work for all of you?" asked Val.

"Yes," said Royale. "With one exception. Why do you need Rafael to run an errand with you?"

"A girl has to have some secrets, baby. You will know soon enough."

"Fasten your seatbelts, everyone," said the captain. "We will be landing in Las Vegas in twenty minutes."

As always, whenever a plane she flew on landed, Val closed her eyes to say a prayer. This time, her request to God was slightly different.

"Please, Father, let my loved ones and I get out of Las Vegas alive."

CHAPTER THIRTY

A Brawl at The Bar

ALTHOUGH IT WAS EARLY AFTERNOON, the scene at the
Three Points Sports Bar, on the westside of Las Vegas, was on
and popping. Jamal sat at the bar, waiting for Aurora to arrive.
He had tried with all his power to get Vance to come with him,
but Mr. Money Bags told him that Rome said he had to stay put
at the hotel until he arrived. Aurora getting to him would have
to wait until the ceremony.

"Didn't I see you at Valerie Rollins' house on Saturday
afternoon?" asked a fine woman with long red locs, sitting next
to him.

"I was there, but I don't remember meeting you. You are too
gorgeous for me not to have noticed you! Please allow me to
introduce myself to you. My name is Jamal. I am a member of
the Dumas Diamonds Polo Club."

"Oh, Vance's polo team. I am Turquoise Hobson. I was
engaged to Rome Nyland. Hopefully, like Jennifer Lopez and

Ben Affleck, we will get back together. At least we are talking about it. What brings you to Las Vegas?"

"Rome is my man," said Jamal. "I flew out to do some fast business with my manager, but I am also attending Vance's wedding this evening."

"Vance is getting married? Is the bride one of the girls I saw him with on Saturday?"

"No. I just met his fiancé last night, which is only a few days less than Vance has known the woman. Her name is Johnyce. It was love at first sight for them. She is fine as hell though."

At that moment, accompanied by two burly young guys, Aurora made a grand entrance into the restaurant. She was wearing a sequined face mask with matching sunglasses and a black dress with sequined sleeves. Her shoes, which were Alexander McQueen Punk Spike Halter Pumps, were also black with studs on them. Ignoring Jamal, she headed to a back booth with her small entourage rushing behind her.

"So, what are you doing in town, beautiful lady?" Jamal asked Turquoise.

"I'm just out here for some rest and relaxation. I decided to check out this spot because it is owned by Royale Jones. I am very curious about him. I am not a big baseball fan, so I didn't know much about him when he was playing baseball. Looking at all this Los Angeles Wildcats memorabilia, I see he was a huge star. There are so many trophies and plaques on the walls and shelves."

Like magic, as soon as Turquoise uttered those words Royale, Rome, Rafael, and Valerie walked in followed by Valerian, Kahari, and two men Turquoise had never seen before. She almost fell off the bar stool at the sight of all of them together.

"Turquoise! Jamal! What are you two doing here together!" exclaimed Valerie.

"Your story seems to stay the same from coast-to-coast, Turquoise," said Rome.

Valerian approached the bar and draped his arm around Turquoise.

"And to think you probably ran way out here to get away from me. As I told you back in the Hamptons, that will never happen, my sweet!"

Removing his hand from around her shoulders, Turquoise addressed Rome.

"I needed to get away and be alone so I could think clearly. Jamal and I met just now at the bar. I came over here because I heard Royale owned it, and I still don't know if I believe he isn't Rolondo."

"Turquoise, I can assure you that I am Royale. Rolondo has been dead four years."

Raven, the restaurant's barmaid, was as shocked as Turquoise to see Royale standing there. This was the first time he had set foot inside of the establishment in almost ten years. He relied on the manager, and her boyfriend, Simeon, to manage everything. This was going to be a problem because the two of them had been skimming money off the top, and there was also a group of Bugatti Blades having a meeting downstairs who were divvying up drug profits.

"It is such a pleasure to see you, Royale. Why didn't you let Simeon know you were coming to town? We would have had something special planned for you. Let me get you all a table. What is everybody drinking?"

"Did you forget that I own this place? I do not have to give you guys advance notice that I am stopping by. We will all sit down in those two booths toward the back. Please let Simeon know that I am here. I do not have time to really handle any business right now, but tomorrow I am going to need to meet with him privately."

Aurora watched what was happening in front of her with awe because luck was surely with her today. The person she hated most in the world, Sincere, stood less than ten feet away from her.

Time had been good to the bastard because he was handsome as ever. She heard him tell Raven he would have a double shot of Jack Daniels straight up. This would be his last drink. His life was about to be over.

"Isn't that our founder, Sincere Davidson, at the bar?" asked Marvin, a newly minted member of the Bugatti Blades.

"Yes, it most certainly is," said Aurora. "I'm going to slip out the side door. I want you two to go over there, order a drink, begin to argue, then start throwing fists at each other." Handing Leonard, a small gun underneath the table, Aurora continued. "While everyone at the bar is focusing on breaking up your fight, move close enough to him, then shoot him. This piece has a silencer on it. Then get out of here before anyone realizes that Sincere has been hit."

Aurora got up quickly, making a fast exit toward the nearest door, not noticing Valerie was focused on her sunglasses.

"Rome, that woman who just walked out of here is wearing a pair of rhinestone sunglasses just like the woman in the picture with Georgette had on. She is also about the same height."

Before Rome had a chance to react, the two guys who had been sitting with the woman, started shoving each other back and forth.

"Whoa," said Royale. "I am the owner of Three Points, and I am going to have to ask you to leave. You need to take whatever beef you have with each other somewhere else."

"Fuck you, man," said Marvin, as he swung at Royale.

Royale ducked, then threw a right hand at him.

Leonard moved toward Valerian, but had to knock Rafael out of the way to get to him.

Rafael didn't take Leonard shoving him lightly and hit Leonard hard.

In a flash, with the exception of the women, everyone at the bar were embroiled in the all-out brawl. Bartimaeus, who was one of the men with Valerie that Turquoise did not recognize, saw Leonard pull a gun out of his pocket. He tackled him as if he were in the middle of a Detroit Lions' game. Rome also saw the pistol, then snatched it out of Leonard's hand as he hit the ground with Bartimaeus on top of him.

"Who are you, man?" Royale asked Leonard as they stood him up. "Who were you trying to kill?"

Leonard remained silent.

Not wanting to call the police with all the illegal activity going on downstairs, letting Royale know that Leonard and Marvin were members of the Blades, Raven said, "He's a regular, Royale. Just let him go."

"Okay. I will let him go, but only because I am getting married in a few hours and do not have any time to deal with this right now. But I am also going to let you and everyone else that works at the bar go. So, you can go downstairs where I am sure Simeon, and the rest of his crew are hiding out and tell them the Three Points Sports Bar is closed for good! It is time to put this place behind me."

He turned his focus back on Marvin and Leonard.

"Can I at least have my gun back?" Leonard asked Rome.

Rome shook his head.

"Not in this lifetime. But before you leave, I need to see your driver's licenses."

Both Marvin and Leonard reluctantly pulled out their wallets, then handed their licenses to Rome, who photographed them.

CHAPTER THIRTY-ONE

Wedding Bells Ring

THE REST of the day passed quickly for Valerie. Standing before the mirror, in her wedding attire, it was hard to process how the grief over Jermonna's death, and the near shooting at Three Points Sports Bar, merged into glee of finally marrying the man of her dreams. Earlier, she had guessed correctly Rafael and Royale wore the same ring size, so he had gone with her to Tiffany's, where she bought a seven-carat wedding band for her groom.

There was a knock on her door, pulling her from her thoughts.

"It's Rome, Val. Are you ready to go to the chapel?"

"Yes, I am," Val called out, opening the door for him and two security guards.

"We are the last to leave, so let's do this," said Rome.

The Venus Gardens Wedding Chapel was right in the Forum Mall at Caesars Palace, so they didn't have far to go. Surrounded by tropical palm trees, a blooming landscape, and

Roman architecture, the garden featured a Roman-styled temple, a relaxing Koi fishpond, a fountain, and unique stone-tiled aisle.

Since the venue was outside, Rome had hired twenty armed security guards to surround the temple.

Each of them had the photo of the mysterious woman with instructions to apprehend anyone who matched her description.

Flanked by more security, Vance, Johnyce, and Royale were already in position when Val and Rome approached the temple at the front of the garden. Val had no idea how Vance had pulled all of this off, but he and Royale wore black, formal tuxedos with tails, while Johnyce was the prettiest bride Valerie had ever seen. Since their lives cloaked with danger, they had made the decision earlier to move through the ceremony quickly.

Val had taken it upon herself to call the Fountain of Hope African Methodist Episcopal Church in Las Vegas to have the head minister marry them. She clutched Royale's hand tightly as Johnyce slipped her arm through Vance's.

"Vance Dumas, will you have Johnyce Parks to be your wife, to live together in holy marriage? Will you love her, comfort her, honor, and keep her in sickness and in health, and forsaking all others, be faithful to her, as long as you both shall live?" asked the pastor.

"I do," said Vance.

The pastor then repeated the vows three times to Johnyce, then to Valerie and Royale, who all answered, "I do."

They all exchanged rings. Between both couples, there had to be enough carats to fill up Harry Winston, Tiffany's, and Van Cleef & Arpels.

"Treat yourselves and each other with respect," said the pastor. "And remind yourselves often of what brought you together. Give the highest priority to the tenderness, gentleness, and kindness that your connection deserves. You have shown your love and affection and have sealed these promises by the giving and receiving of the rings. Therefore, it is my privilege, as a minister, and by the authority given to me by the state of Nevada, I now pronounce that you are husband and wife. Gentlemen, you may kiss your wives."

He did not have to ask Vance or Royale twice.

They kissed their brides with intense passion and love.

The pastor ended the ceremony with, "Ladies and gentlemen, it is my privilege to introduce to you, for the first time, Mr. and Mrs. Dumas along with Mr. and Mrs. Jones."

The sweet solace was savored for a second before Valerian yelled out from the entrance into the gardens. "Andrea!" He pulled off a woman's face mask who had somehow forged her way through the throngs of security guards that now had her in custody. A shot rang out. Valerian crumpled to the ground.

"Yes, you vile bastard. I am Andrea Dumas in the flesh! And you are a dead man!"

CHAPTER THIRTY-TWO

One Month Later
The Monte-Carlo Cup
Monte-Carlo, Monaco

Polo, called The Sport of Kings and the King of Sports, was a well-known unique sport for quite some time. Today, the sport had millions of fans from every corner of the world. Sitting with Johnyce, Royale and Rome, in red velvet throne-like chairs, with a beautifully set table in front of them, Valerie said, "This Monte-Carlo Polo Club has to be the most beautiful place I have ever been."

"It is pretty spectacular," remarked Royale.

Weighing in, Johnyce commented, "I am in disbelief of this new life God has blessed me with. I cannot believe I am sitting among all these professional athletes, celebrities, socialites, and high-class people. I overheard that Prince Albert II and Princess Charlene of Monaco are here somewhere."

"I still find it unbelievable that Andrea was alive all this time and that Valerian is dead. Even though he tortured us for years, I never wished death upon the man. God is still on the throne. Only our Father made sure we were all married before the chaos erupted. And what did killing Valerian do for Andrea? She is still locked up. But instead of being in a rehabilitation facility, she is now in jail, awaiting trial, for the murders of Dwayne, Georgette, and Valerian, not to mention the attempted murders of Vance, Johnyce, and Kwami. Vance and I would have willingly split Dumas Electronics with her. She is Victor's rightful widow," Valerie said.

As they chatted, Vance rode Wildin' Out straight to the goal post, swung out his chukka, and scored the winning goal.

They jumped up, clapping wildly while hugging each other. The Dumas Diamonds Polo Club had just made history, becoming the first all-Black polo team to win the coveted Monte-Carlo Cup! Good always triumphed over evil.

Royale wrapped his arms tightly around Valerie.

"Are you ready to set sail throughout the entire South of France with me tonight, Mrs. Jones?"

She looked deeply into her man's eyes.

"I have been ready since you hit that home run for me forty years ago. I love you, Mr. Jones."

READERS GROUP QUESTIONS

1. Should Valerie have waited four years after her husband, Victor's, death to have sex with her college sweetheart, Royale Jones?
2. Why does Royale love Valerie so much?
3. Is Vance a sex-addicted pig or a player?
4. Have you ever met a Black billionaire?
5. Do you think someone could hide they are still alive for over a decade like Aurora/Andrea did?
6. Why did Vance fall in love with Pastor Johnyce so quickly?
7. Do you believe in love at first sight?
8. Do you think Valerian/Sincere deserved to be killed?

NEW STREET LIT TITLES

FROM WAHIDA CLARK PRESENTS INNOVATIVE PUBLISHING

When he returned their licenses, the two guys scurried out of the bar in a mad rush.

"Why don't you sell the Three Points, cousin?" asked Sincere. "It would be a shame to let a family business close. I have always frequented this place more than you. Being in Las Vegas today has made me realize how much I love this town."

"It is yours if you want it. But for right now the bar is closed. Come on, Sweet Val. It is almost time for us to finally get married. Raven, Sincere and I will see you and Simeon tomorrow to discuss everything that is going on," said Royale.

As Rome got ready to walk out, Turquoise grabbed his hand.

"Where are you staying?" she asked.

"At Caesars Palace. How about you?"

"What a coincidence. I'm there too."

"I don't mean to interrupt, Rome," said Sincere. "Turquoise, I just want you to know that Valerie and I have come to an understanding, so I will not be bothering you anymore. You no longer have to fear me."

"Thank you," said Turquoise.

Still holding her hand, Rome asked, "How did you get here? Do you need a lift back to the hotel?"

"That would be nice. I took an Uber here," said Turquoise.

"Come on. You can ride with us."

She followed him out of the door.

"Are you all right, sweetheart?"" Val asked Royale, as they prepared to leave.

"I am fine. When you retire from football Bartimaeus, you should make wrestling your second career."

Happy to have something to joke about, Bartimaeus told him, "I just might do that, Mr. Royale."

"Valerian," said Val. "I am pretty sure your cousins, Rome, and Bartimaeus saved your life today. I saw a strange woman run out of here just before those guys started fighting. The one with the gun was aiming it at you. Putting two and two together, that woman's aura, sunglasses, and height reminded me of the second woman talking to Jermonna in the bar. Mark my words. She is the mastermind behind all this violence. We have to find out who she is."

"I guess having a family and friends may not be such a bad thing after all," said Sincere.

Listening to Valerie, Jamal realized it was only a matter of time before they discovered Andrea was still alive. It was time for him to distance himself from her. He owed his career as a jockey, and now successful polo player, to Victor and Vance. The world was his oyster. He was not going to ruin his life for a woman that used him as a sex toy.

He followed the New York crew out to the parking lot. Getting into his rented SUV, he said, "I will see you all at the wedding."

Hidden behind a column, Aurora was outraged that for the second time in two days, her plans to kill Vance and Sincere had failed. While Valerie did not know who she was, the bitch was somewhat on to her. Since explosions and guns didn't kill Sincere or Vance, she was going back to her first plan of taking Valerie and Vance's money. Like Jamal, she would see all of them later at the wedding.